My Heart on Your Sleeve

April Klasen

Independently Published
2025

First Printing: 2025

Paperback ISBN 978-1-923217-00-3
E-book ISBN 978-1-923217-01-0

April Klasen

Acknowledgements

Thank you to **Abby Cox** over on Youtube for their fabulous content on historical costuming. I have learned a lot! And this story wouldn't exist without watching a video where they were talking about mantua makers and feminism and ranting about the rise of the modern fashion industry. And I think it was them that mentioned something about how so many historical romances are written for the high society of an era and rarely for the working class and so perpetuates stereotypes about history, which I took as a challenge for myself. If it wasn't them who said that, then I am sorry to the person who did, I didn't mean to forget.

As always, thank you **Mother** for your proofreading.

Dedicated to my great-great-granny.

1. I Think I ~~Like~~ Love You

"Stop!"

"It's not me."

"Then who else is it?" She shushed me. But it broke off with that light little giggle of hers. "You're doing it."

"I am not," I defended my honour. But then giggled along with her. *Tehehe.*

"You're tickling me every time," she playfully showed me just how I was meant to be tickling by thrusting her wiggling fingers under my chin.

Catching me off guard, I squealed.

"Girls," our mentor, Mrs Herrick, called our attention as she looked up from her work. "Are you getting any draping done or are you playing with each other?"

Oh Lord! Don't say it like that! We're not those sorts of girls.

"Sorry, ma'am," we both said at the same time. Good and obedient. Our laughter stifled down into our chests, fighting to come back up through our throats so hard we shook with the effort to hold it in. Her brown cheeks flushed darker, matching how hot my face felt.

"Hmm," Mrs Herrick rolled her eyes at us and went back to her whip stiches.

Us however, looked at each other and instantly lost it. I snorted, that's how my laugh broke through. And her? Well, she held her giggle behind her hand and turned away from me to release a loud and obnoxious *pfft*.

The others in the work room all scoffed and carried on with their work. Sixteen women and girls in total filled the space. All of us employed by Mrs Herrick. Six of us were apprenticing under her. The others were her full-fledged mantua makers all working on gowns for our lady customers.

They moved about the workspace doing various tasks. Some sat cross legged on the large table under the full windows and had their work laid over pillows on their laps, or on stools at the long bench by the other window, happily stitching away as they chatted with one another.

Others were using the cutting tables to cut long rectangular lengths of fabrics that would be pleated down onto the waist ties and become skirts for the gowns. Or measuring out the large amounts of trim needed to edge their masterpieces with frills and lace and ribbons.

Then there was us. I was sixteen and nearing the end of my apprenticeship. Hopefully. And right then I was practicing the art of draping on my model.

Her.

Isa.

Also sixteen and close to finishing her apprenticeship alongside me. She was pretty. Beautiful. Skin a deep tan, along with dark curling locks that escaped her pins on a regular as the work day passed. And she would do battle with to comb each evening and morning.

"Anne," Isa snapped her fingers right in my face to get my attention.

I grimaced and slapped her hand away. "What?"

"Well, it's not exactly warm standing here like this," she swung her hands out to show off her current state of undress; stays, chemise, petticoats and stockings. Only she added in a little flirty cock of her brow and tilt of her head as she did. That said something else. Something like, *'look at me, pay attention to me.'*

Or maybe I was reading too much into all of this.

I placed my hands on her shoulders and turned her away from me, my face burning as I did… and touch lingering on her bare skin, just a little. Just a moment. I couldn't help it. "I'm trying to work. But you keep on squirming."

"That's because you're tickling me," she turned to fire over her shoulder.

I glared at her. "I am trying to drape this to get it to fit to your body. It's not my fault that I have to touch you."

"You're doing it too gently," she complained.

Was I? Was I doing it differently to how I normally did it with anyone else? Oh Lord, please no. I do not want think of the last time I draped, because that had been on Mrs Herrick and surely I hadn't touched her the same. Right?

"Anne," Isa complained again. "Stop teasing me," she giggled.

"Teasing you? What a laugh," but this time I did tease. I made sure as I pinned the piece in the back to her stays to get it to hold in place, that I dragged my fingertips over her exposed neck.

She squirmed. Goose flesh erupting over her.

"Stop moving, I'm about to cut," I warned. And did a similar action with the edge of the scissors as I began to cut the fabric now resting on her skin. Knowing full well how it felt to have them run along you. How it made you shiver with the fear of being snipped.

Isa inhaled sharply.

I bit my lip and focussed on my task, on following the natural curve of her body as I cut the piece. Then pinned another layer of fabric beside that piece and smoothed it out and cut it to fit. Repeat. All around her torso. From back, to under her arms, to front.

And *whoa*... that might've been a mistake.

Shit.

She was bitting her lip. High on her cheeks was that dark blush again. And her chest was moving a lot with her fast breath. Rise and fall.

"Like what you see?" Isa bit her lip.

What?

"I haven't draped anything yet," I forced out.

She smirked. "I know."

Oh hell. Oh bloody hell. What was I... how?! How was I to respond to that? Was this even friendly banter any-more.

And...

What is wrong with me? It never was a difficulty before to drape a bodice onto someone. To be so up and close in their space, touching areas that wasn't acceptable in any other context. Even the times Isa and I had practiced before, it hadn't been like this. And we joked around then. We'd giggled and teased.

But now? Now I'm hyper aware.

Aware of her in her undergarments. In the way she moved around each time she shifted. In her smiles and glimmer in her eyes.

And her comments.

They were the same as before, the type of outrageous words to make us laugh.

So why were they different sounding now? Like, she meant them more. Or I wanted her to mean them more.

She started to frown at me.

Oh no. I reached up and pinched her nose between my fingers and complained. "You are being annoying," I told her. "A model needs to not distract an artiste as they try to work."

"Hey," she slapped my hands. Then reached up to grab my nose and hold it in place too. "I'm not doing anything different! And who are you calling artiste?! Huh? You're an apprentice just like me."

We glared, holding each other's noses and playing some ridiculous game of chicken.

"Anne, Isa," Mrs Herrick called.

Ah shit.

With one last squeeze of my nose, she released me. I followed her lead and did the same.

"Sorry, ma'am," came out automatically.

"As entertaining as it is to watch the two of you flirt, you're both at work currently," the older woman fixed us with her most disappointing stare and we both hunched our shoulders a little more in response. "You cannot act like this in front of clients."

"Sorry, ma'am."

She tapped her nail against the worn wooden table she sat upon and stared at us. Assessing. "How much more do you need to do to finish the draping process, Anne?"

"Just the front panels of the bodice, sleeves, and the measurements for the skirts." Ten minutes if we didn't distract each other and I stopped having my little mental crisis.

"Hmm. Last chance girls."

We were warned. And turned back to each other and continued on with very little teasing. Very sombre and to the point. I pinned on the fabric over Isa's chest, using her stays as a solid base. Cut out the shapes. Smoothed it all out. Used tailors chalk to number each piece and removed them, stacking them onto the table beside me.

Isa was the perfect model. Lifting her arms as I requested. Standing still. Pulling faces at me. I snipped the scissors threateningly in front of her nose. She rolled her eyes and mouthed out an insult. Perfect model.

Next up, I took a length of paper tape and wrapped it around her waist. Marked each point with little cuts on it. Where the sides of the skirt would sit. The length of the ties to be comfortable for her to fasten them closed in the back and in the front. Length of skirt.

She watched me, closely. All with her teasing little smile. When I passed my arms around behind her back to get the waist measurement she lifted her brows up in a comedic suggestive way. "Getting familiar there, Anne," she purred.

"Prefer me to be cold and distant, Isa?" I fired back.

She settled her hands onto my waist. "No. I like this." And there was something honest in her tone as she said that. No more flirting.

My heart raced in my chest. I swallowed hard. My eyes darting away to see if Mrs Herrick or if anyone else that was bustling around the work room was paying attention to us. No. Looking back, Isa smiled at me.

I... *what*...

I dipped my head and stepped away. Taking my pencil to write out Isa's name onto the paper tape and add it to my stack of pattern pieces.

I cleared my throat. "You can get dressed again." This time, I couldn't look at her. "I've got everything I need."

"Do you?" She started to slide her clothes on over her under garments. Covering up once more.

"What else am I missing?" I snapped back.

A beat of silence. "Nothing. I guess."

And there it was, destroyed. Whatever little flirtation we'd been sharing was gone in the matter of seconds it took for me to say stupid shit and for her to give up on me. And I had no clue as to how to get it back to where we had been.

So, I turned to Mrs Herrick and announced being finished with my draping.

Isa stuck the last of her straight pins into her bodice to hold it closed and her heels clicked as she walked away and back to her little work station and the gown she'd been working on.

I sighed.

Mrs Herrick chuckled. Indulgent. "Did you have your model pick out a fabric?"

Oh shit. I had forgotten something.

"Isa!" I called out to her.

*

The dorm room was always noisy. With six apprentices ranging in ages from twelve to twenty, it was busy. Laughter. Arguments. Gossip.

Cot beds lining either side of the room. Trunks at the end of them filled with our belongings.

I undressed slowly. Taking out the pins holding shut my bodice over my stays, putting them carefully to the side so I didn't lose any. Sighing as I was able to shrug out of it. And then loosening the ties of my over skirt and then the petticoats and my pockets. *Fuck.* The pockets weighed a lot.

They clattered as I dropped them to the top of my trunk. My small sewing kit inside of it, scissors, purse, key to my trunk, etc. My world fitted into my pockets. But that didn't mean they were light and easy to carry around all of the time.

"Anne!" The only warning I had before Isa crashed into me and hugged me from behind. Her chin resting on my shoulder. "Need some help?" her fingers played with the lacings in the front of my stays.

I didn't shrug her off. "Are you helpful?" I tossed back to her.

She dipped her fingers under the edge of the stays, and drew out the knot and tails of my lacing. "I can be," she teased.

No touch grazed skin. It was careful. She undid the knot. Loosened the spiral.

I breathed and relaxed into her, my back resting against her chest, so I felt her chuckle. It rocked through me.

"Better?" Isa asked.

"It's nice to take it off at the end of the day," I admitted.

"Hmm, it sure is," but she sounded distracted.

I tried to look at her, but we were too close together, I only got the view of her cheek and could gather she was looking down… her fingers twirled the tails of the lacing.

"What?"

"Huh?" now she turned to face me, nose bumping me. She pulled back. "What?"

We stared.

I swallowed. "Nothing." *What was I doing? What was going on here?* Stepping away, I finished removing my stays and placed them onto the trunk as well.

My chemise finally billowed out and around. "I'm going to wash up," I announced.

"Okay," Isa went to the cot beside mine, her cot, and bounced as she sat down onto it.

I went to the corner of the room with the privacy screen set up. Surprised one of the other girls using the chamber pot. "Hey, privacy!" she squawked at me.

I turned and went and waited by the corner of the screen. God, this living situation sucked.

Once behind the screen was free again, I went to the hip basin and used a cloth there to scrub my hands and face. Poured fresh water from the pitcher to rinse. Steadied myself.

It wasn't like we were acting any differently.

In the last four years we'd been working and living and studying together, we'd always been the same. We'd have a laugh. Fight. Get over it. Hung off of each other. So why was this feeling… different?

"Are you almost finished?" Someone poked their head around the corner. "I need to wash up."

I nodded and came around the screen, leaving it to her. I went back out and stopped at Isa's cot and dropped down beside her.

She was talking to the girl who slept on her other side, Mary. They were discussing tomorrow. I didn't really care or pay attention, just leant in and rested my head on her shoulder. Not pausing, she moved and wrapped her arm around me and drew me in tight.

"It's going to be so much fun," she announced.

The girl, she was one of the older ones, Mary, looked between the two of us with a frown.

"What?" Isa asked.

"Nothing," Mary responded. "Are you two together?"

Isa snorted. "No. What are you on about?"

I didn't respond. She was stroking up and down my arm, and her other hand had taken mine from my lap and moved it to hers, threading our fingers.

Even Mary was looking at us like she didn't believe the words out of Isa's mouth. "Are you sure you're not? Because… well," she pointed at us. "And the way you two were flirting with one another in the work room."

Isa scoffed. "That wasn't flirting. Right Anne?"

It wasn't? "Hmm." *Then what the hell was it? Was it two girls being friendly?*

Mary shook her head. "Doesn't matter. But we have a plan for tomorrow."

"That we do," Isa vibrated under my head with her excitement. She gripped my fingers. "You're coming with us Anne."

I groaned and turned to hide my face into her shoulder. "Nooooo."

"Yeeeeessss!" she cried out. "You have to."

"But I don't wanna," I complained.

Mary laughed. "You want to miss out on all of the fun?"

What fun? It was a stupid dance at the public hall. They held them monthly for the public. The last one hadn't been fun. Nor the one before that. Isa and I were old enough for Mrs Herrick to give us permission to attend with the other older girls. I wished it was the year before and we had to be in bed before curfew and miss out on the nonsense.

I grunted. And pouted.

Isa dropped a kiss to the top of my head and cuddled me close. "It won't so bad."

Yes, it would be. It would be the same as last time and I didn't want to do that again.

Ever.

"Lights out, ladies," Mrs Herrick announced from the doorway.

There was a general groaning in protest. A couple of them begging for five minutes more. But Mrs Herrick ignored and went about extinguishing the few candles we'd burned, taking the last remaining one out with her and closing the door solidly after.

We all slipped into our own beds.

I settled onto my side and looked over into the darkness at Isa. She reached across the distance to grab my hand. "Hey," she whispered.

I squeezed her fingers back. "What?"

"You don't have to come to the dance… if you don't want to," she admitted.

I could hear the pout in her voice. Knew what she would look like with it. How her bottom lip would protrude and there would be a tinge of disappointment overall in her face.

"You promise not to abandon me this time?" I tried to hope for her to actually hold that promise as a solemn oath. One that has to be followed.

"I won't abandon you… but you don't like dancing. And I do. I want to go to dance."

Dance with boys.

There it was! The truth of it all. Isa was popular with the tradesmen who came to these public dances. With the young lads who cleaned themselves up to come and talk to a pretty girl, spin her about the dance floor, and maybe steal a kiss if not their heart.

And I didn't like any of them. They would come up to us, find the other girls easy to chat with, but not me. Oh no. I was clear in my dislike of them.

I wanted to dance too. With Isa. Not with those boys.

"Hmm," I rolled to my back and stared at the darkened ceiling. Still holding hands with Isa.

"Maybe you'd like it too if you tried to dance with someone," she ventured.

"Go to sleep," from across the room was grumbled.

Isa untangled her hand from mine and withdrew. "Sleep tight."

"Don't let the bed bugs bite," I finished with a sigh.

Soon enough, she was passed out. Along with the rest of the girls in the room, told by the snoring of a couple, and no shifting around to find a comfortable position.

But I stayed awake.

It was odd. We weren't different, she wasn't different with me. It was the same and yet… and yet I couldn't stop myself from gravitating towards Isa. From wanting to touch her. Anything from teasing pinches to looping our arms together to sitting thigh to thigh. And brightened under her returned affection.

But…

It was a moment. A realisation. Going from before to knowing and realising that I loved Isa. I was in love with Isa.

That maybe I hadn't always been so, but I was right then.

And the worst of it all, she didn't love me.

Loved me as a friend, sure. As someone she could confide in and kiss on the cheek.

My head turned and I stared at her in the dark. Her lying on her side, hand flopped out and dangling over the edge of the cot. Hair in her loose sleeping braid. Sheet dipping low.

I wanted to reach over and pull it back up for her. Tuck her in. Kiss her temple goodnight.

Dear God, I am in love with her. And it settled heavy into my chest, like a weight. *Fuck. No.* I didn't want to be in love with my best friend.

I rolled over to the other side and stared at the wall.

Maybe she was right and I should try to dance with someone tomorrow night.

"How do I look?"

"Good."

"Yeah, but do I look pretty?"

I rolled my eyes. "Isa. You are pretty. Always pretty." I admitted.

Isa smiled. Soft. Her steps slowed. She leaned in and planted a quick kiss to my cheek. Then laughed. "Oops."

I stopped in the middle of the entry to the dance hall. I knew what she'd done. *Ugh.* "Stop getting it on me!" I complained.

Her lip stain that her and the other girls had painted on together in the dorm room mirror, was a vibrant and sticky red. Made from beetroot powder and oil. Some had dabbed it to their cheeks as well. Luckily, they'd learned their lesson with me and didn't even offer to smear it over my lips.

It had felt awful the one time I'd tried it. I didn't like it. And it got everywhere. I think I ate more of it than wore.

The other girls all chuckled as they watched Isa fetch out her handkerchief and wiped. Only to smear it and have to dampen the fabric with her spit and try again.

"Should've left it on," Mary teased. "Then maybe she'd attract some looks from those types of women."

I frowned at that.

Another girl elbowed Mary in the ribs. Mary apologised and brushed it off. She was rosy cheeked. But not because of any more make up. No. Because of a secret bottle of liquor that was passed around before we left. That was still stashed in someone's pocket.

"You look good," Isa leant in and whispered into my ear.

The crowd crowded in on us. We'd entered the dance hall. I grabbed her hand and gripped hard. She squeezed back.

Music from the small platform at the front of the hall was lively. And loud. People talked and laughed and shouted. From my left, a man raised his voice and his hand that held a cup, only for its contents to slosh over and come down onto my arm.

Bastard.

"Oh, beggin' ya sorry, miss," he laughed.

Isa laughed along with him and mopped up the spill as best she could with her handkerchief.

I wanted to go home.

Then it was a whirl. Boys came. We were all spilt up. Something something. *Oh look, Isa let go of my hand and was off on the dance floor.* And I was miserable standing against the wall and trying not to attract attention.

Must've been working. My face pulled into a sour pout. No boys came near. Small blessings.

But it was boring to stand there and watch my friends. *Lord, I'm a wet blanket.* But honestly, could you blame me? The lads were… not for me. I didn't find any of them appealing.

None.

I was shocked to find that my eyes strayed from Isa to look at the women… *oh my.* There were some very pretty women in the crowd. Some who rivalled Isa and I really liked her.

Love, yes. But I'm trying not to hope for the impossible.

So my eyes wandered over the women and I marvelled at them. But did nothing. Because though I looked, none of them returned the look back at me. I hadn't caught any-one's attention.

*

I had wanted to leave after an hour. But we'd stayed until the wee hours, until the hall closed and we were all kicked out onto the streets to stumble home.

One lad had been attached to Isa all night. And as he offered to walk us back, his eyes trained only on Isa.

I took note of the smear of lipstick on the corner of his mouth.

"I want to make sure, you ladies get home safe," he told her.

Isa bit her lip and looked over her shoulder.

Mary nodded. As did the others. I pretended to be too tired and not paying attention.

"We'd be honoured," she said as she turned back to him. "To have your company on our walk back."

He grinned this boyish grin. Offered her his arm and took the lead with her. So we could all trail behind and keep an eye on them. Chaperon. At three in the morning. *Ugh.*

He was tall, broad shouldered in the way of an adult. *He must be older than us.* Isa looked tiny beside him.

Height wise. Her small waist. She was sixteen. Not yet fully grown up.

She laughed at what he was whispering to her as they walked. Had to be shushed because it was too loud for the street so late at night.

Mary bumped into me. "You alright there?"

"Hmm," I grunted.

"You gonna make a fuss?"

At that, I shot her a glare. "No."

She laughed. Still rosy from alcohol and from the fun night. Slung her arm over my shoulder and dragged me to join the rest of the group who all stumbled and laughed and *oh hell*, got me to smile and laugh along with them.

Like it was a contagion.

We started to chant some bawdy song we should never had heard. It was fun. More fun than standing around the edge of the dance hall and waiting for the night to end.

My arm wrapped around Mary's waist.

We were in a line and doing these little synchronised kicks down the street, the heels of our shoes click clacking in time, when we arrived home. Then it was all shushing so we didn't disturb Mrs Herrick or the rest of the girls.

Someone had a key and opened the door. We filed in. I hesitated and looked over to Isa and the young man, off to the side. Eyes only for each other as they spoke their last few words.

"Isa," Mary whisper shouted. She tossed her head towards the door.

Isa, blush high in her cheeks, nodded, turned back and spoke to him one last time before leaving him there. Looked over her shoulder before going through the door.

I followed. Mary closed and locked up.

And yeah.

Isa collapsed onto me and started to babble away. "Oh my Lord! Did you see him? Did you see that man?! He was so handsome! And… ahh!" she dissolved into a giggle and buried her head into my neck. Uncontrollably shaking in her excitement.

I endured it.

She pulled back. "Anne!" she hissed. "I think I'm in love!"

Mary saved me. "Be in love upstairs," she ordered and reached over my shoulder to give Isa a shove. "Go on."

Isa stumbled and danced up the stairs on her toes, all in an attempt to soften her footsteps.

I wanted to stomp. *Thud thud.* Direct some of this… what? Jealousy? Rage? Hatred for a man I knew nothing of?

The dorm was dimly lit. The young girls were rumpled as they lifted their heads to tell us to be quiet. And everyone was trying to be. With lots of shushing and giggling as they struggled out of clothes and collapsed onto beds. Sometimes taking a friend down with them.

I hurried to the privacy screen to wash up first. *Love? Isa was in love after one night? How was that possible when it took me years to be in love with her?!*

*

"He's twenty-one," Isa whispered to me. "And he's here on a business trip. His family runs a printing press up north."

I nodded along to her words, not daring to risk a verbal response. We were seated side by side as we worked. Or, I worked and she seemed to getting all stary eyed and running her mouth about him.

Knew he was older.

I kept my stitches even along the seam of the gown I was making. Her gown. This was for Isa and it was my assignment I was going to be showing to Mrs Herrick for her approval. So I had to be careful with it. Make sure I didn't fuck it up by throwing a huge hissy fit and tossing it into the fire while I screamed.

The rich red colour she'd chosen was going to complement her skin beautifully.

"It was so nice of him to walk us home, last night," she continued. "Such manners."

"Do you think this young man will come a courtin'?" One of the older ladies called over from her side of the table.

Yes, everyone was having the absolute fun torture of hearing Isa gush because though she whispered, she was the only one talking and filling the air with a voice. "I… um," she blushed and dipped her head. A sad smile now on the edge of her lips. "I would like to hope so. But I don't know."

The older ladies all chuckled and consoled her.

"Men are fickle."

"As long as you didn't give a proper taste, he'll be back for more."

"If not, plenty more men out there for ya."

Isa sighed. Wistful.

He did come courting. He came by the shop with flowers. He was invited in for tea and sat beside Isa, and though we were all there, we didn't exist between the two. They talked and laughed and made plans to see each other the next day.

And I watched it all.

An afternoon became a week of visits, became two, became letters and presents.

And then…

"He proposed!" Isa burst into the dorm room and squealed.

Everyone started to squeal and congratulate her. They swarmed her and gave her hugs and kisses to her cheeks.

Even I did. Just to fit in. So it wasn't obvious that my heart was broken. "Congratulations," I pecked her cheek.

She squeezed me back hard and held on tight. "I'm getting married," she laughed and started to dance me around the room. "I'm getting married!"

*

She wore my dress. The one I'd made for her, had draped on her while we were giggling and having the best of times. Yeah. That dress. She wore it to marry him.

The dress with the fitted half sleeves that flared out with a ruff on the end. Low cut bodice with a contrasting trim along the neckline. I had gotten it to be perfectly flat, not a wrinkle in sight on the fabric. And yards of skirt. An English gown. Even the pleats on the back were perfect. Uniform.

She'd looked beautiful.

Hair pulled back, little ringlets framing her face. A touch of blush and lip stain.

Mrs Herrick loaned her a necklace. Had fluffed around. Straitening things. Looking over Isa's shoulder to smile at her in the mirror. "A lovely bride," she'd told her.

Isa had been grinning like mad.

The rest of us, fluttered around getting ready in the dorm. Our best dresses to be paraded down the street to the church.

I waited on Isa hand and foot. Not because I truly wanted. But because she had been sneaky and made me promise her a favour before asking me to be her maid of honour.

Oh, what an honour it was to help the one I loved get ready to marry another! Pah!

"Cloak," I announced as I draped the thing over her shoulders, clasping it in the front and settling the hood up and over her hair with the greatest of care.

She pinched my nose. "What is it?" she asked, still with a smile.

"What?" that caught me off guard. Smacked her away out of habit.

"You're off," she said. "Is something wrong?"

"No," I automatically answered. "Everything's fine."

Silence. I turned to make sure I had all of the little items in my pocket to help fix up her appearance once we got her to the church. So many things could go wrong and we needed to be prepared. Combs, pins, sewing kits, lip stains, pocket mirrors.

"Ready?" I asked the girls in the dorm. Received a number of answers from yes to almost to complaining about stolen gloves. "Then out the door," I ordered. Mrs Herrick led them. Counting them off as they passed by her.

Isa grabbed my wrist. "Anne," she started.

"We don't have time to dilly dally," I told her. Firm. We didn't. If we didn't leave then and there we would be late to the ceremony. "Whatever it is can wait."

Isa grimaced, then nodded and allowed her face to break into a smile once more.

But she didn't release my wrist. Only switched to holding my hand as she stood and left the dorm by my side.

*

They married.

Isa was married.

She was a man's wife.

Changed her family name.

No longer slept in the dorm with the rest of us girls. She slept in the small room her husband had rented for the time he was in town doing business.

Her old cot was an empty gap.

*

"What do you mean, Isa?" I demanded.

She sighed and sank onto her old cot, as if she'd never left and it was still hers. "You heard what I said." She seemed tired.

But that wasn't something I could notice right then. I was angry. Livid. "You're giving up your apprenticeship?! With not even a year left? If that!"

"I'm going home with my husband. He's been away for too long."

"Then he can go and you can stay and finish what you bloody well started!" I snapped back.

She'd come to visit Mrs Herrick that morning. Not come to work. They'd gone into her office.

None of us in the work room knew what was happening. Why would Isa and Mrs Herrick be talking? Had something happened? We buzzed with it. Gossiped over it and watched the closed door. Until it opened and Mrs Herrick looked at me and jerked her chin to the stairs to our living quarters.

I had followed Isa up. She'd taken us to the dorm and had told me the news.

She was going to leave her apprenticeship as a mantua maker and follow her husband back to his family's home in the north. She was leaving.

I fumed. "What a laugh," I sneered. "You get married and suddenly nothing else in your life matters."

"Enough," she leapt to her feet and glared at me. "It was my choice in the end."

I held back any other cutting remark I wanted to make. Of her losing her independence to him by this. She would not be a qualified mantua maker. She could take on work, sure, but it wouldn't be with the full qualification.

"You're becoming a dressmaker," she sighed and sank back down to the cot. "Not because you like making dresses."

I gritted my teeth. "You know why I'm doing this." The independence and security of being able to provide for myself and not rely on others. To have my own trade and be proud of it!

"Exactly," she said. "And you know exactly why I was doing it. But now, I'm getting to live out a new dream of mine. I get to be a wife and have a family," she twisted her skirt in her grip. Anxious.

I tried to stay true to my anger and not give in. But… I couldn't. I went and slumped down beside her on that small cot. "I don't like it."

"You don't have to," she admitted.

My head plopped sideways to her shoulder and she dropped an affectionate kiss to my hair.

"I can always come back to it, if I want to."

"Hmm," I pouted. "When do you leave?"

"Next week."

So soon?

She reached over and took my hand. Cradled it in her lap.

Damn it. Why did she have to go and make it so… hard?

With my free hand, I swiped at my cheeks. Dashing away the fresh tears that seemed to have sprung free. I sniffled.

She pulled me into a hug and held me as I cried. "I'll miss you too," she whispered.

I clung tight to her.

*

One last bloody dance. I dressed along with the other girls in the dorm and we traipsed across town to the dance hall. It was the last dance that Isa would dance at with us and I couldn't for the life of me find a reason to avoid it.

The crowd was large and rowdy. So much noise. Mary spotted Isa first. She called to her and waved. Isa lit up as she saw us and waved for us to cross the room to her. She was in her husband's company.

Hugs exchanged.

Something something happened. And then they were on the dance floor. All of the girls had a partner. Isa was twirling around with her husband and laughing as they did so.

And I was on the wall again.

I watched and hated that this would be the last time I would see her. Maybe. Or maybe I would go and see her off before she left. Or maybe she would stop by the shop to say goodbye. No matter what, it was the end and I hated it and why the devil was I torturing myself with this?!

The crowd shuffled and bumped into me. I moved along the wall. Further and further until I was stepping around and through a doorway and…

Space.

It was darkened. Not in use for the evening.

I sighed and leaned against the wall, tried not to lose it. Slipped down. Sat there, knees drawn up. Would it be alright for me to leave now? I'd seen her. She saw me. It wouldn't be like she would come and look for me anyway, not when she had her husband there and he was the centre of her universe now.

"Oh," a surprised voice made me lift my head. And there was a woman I recognised. A milliner. She sold to the shop.

"Miss Thompson?"

She grinned at that. "Kitty. Please. Miss Thompson is my sister."

I smiled, polite, and nodded to her.

She edged away from the door. Stood beside me, so her skirts were against my arm. It was a lovely fabric, a taffeta. Would cost a small fortune. My fingers reached out and stroked it.

"You're one of Mrs Herrick's girls, right?" in her hand she had a goblet.

"Yes. I'm an apprentice."

We lapsed into silence. The only sound coming from the other room.

She sipped her goblet.

If I stood up, would it be rude if I left her there? But then again, she was the one to intrude on my solitude, so I think I should be allowed to sit there and expect her to leave first.

"Not interested in boys?" she asked.

I looked up. Noted that she was looking at me and then looking away. She was… rather pretty. I smiled and shook my head. "No."

"Interested in girls?" she asked, casual. As if it was something someone could ask a stranger.

I blushed. I had never had to admit it out loud to another person before. But looking at her. And considering the way she inquired, and how she glanced at me again… as if she was assessing things.

I looked her up and down. *Why not? Not like I had a chance with someone else's wife.* "Are you?" I asked. Bold. Trying my best to sound flirtatious. To look up at her from under my lashes.

Must've worked, she smiled and offered her wine goblet to me.

I accepted and drank deep, maintaining eye contact.

"Want to find out?" she teased back.

"Yes." *Yes I did.* I scrambled to my feet. She reached out and steadied me with hands on my waist. I laughed, self-conscious.

We slipped back into the hall and headed towards the powder room, but dipped off and down a hallway. She tugged me into a secluded corner.

Biting her lip she pressed me against the wall and leaned into me. My eyes zeroed in on her mouth. Wanted to…

Her lips broke into a grin. "Have you ever kissed a girl?"

I shook my head.

"Do you want to?"

I nodded.

Then she kissed me.

My hands came up and held her face.

Dear Lord, she was kissing me. And I enjoyed it. Loved it. Moved my lips under hers to mimic the way she did. When her tongue swiped, I opened my mouth. I tasted her wine.

Her hand hiked up my skirts and went under. The hem of it, my petticoats, and chemise all gathered and sitting on her forearm while she touched me. First my thigh. Gentle and teasing. And closer and closer.

"Huh," my breath hitched.

She grinned against my mouth.

She fingered me. Every few strokes changed, like she was testing it all out until this time, I moaned. "Ahhh," I dropped my forehead to her bare collarbone and panted against the skin there. Felt her light chuckle.

"Found it," she said and kept her fingers right there, stroking.

I grabbed her arms and squeezed hard. Rolled my face into the crook of her neck and mouthed at the skin there.

I came. After some time.

She laughed into my ear, kissed my temple.

My skirts dropped back down. "Whoa," I tried to catch my breath. Lifted my face and kissed her back.

"My turn," she prompted. Guiding my hand to under her skirt.

I fumbled. Needed direction. My hand cramped. But she moaned into my ear.

I flipped our positions, made her lean against the wall and I rested my weight onto her. She liked that. Hiked her leg up and over my hip, dragged me in closer still. "There," she hissed. Clenched down on my fingers. "Right there!" Her hips moved, grinding against my palm.

And then she came, head back and eyes closed.

I put my head back down to the crook of her neck again and hid. Let her ride it out until she directed me to stop and withdraw.

We kissed. Slow and sloppy.

And then she left me.

3. The Years Keep Coming

Fourteen years later…

"I swear to God, Easther!" I gritted my teeth and glared at my employee. "You're testing my patience."

Eather just cackled away and continued on with her bloody teasing.

I should fire her. To hell with it. Why did I put up with such blatant disrespect from a damn apprentice? I had never been this unprofessional when I had been an apprentice! It was this new generation of kids.

"What's wrong, boss," she smiled. "Did I say something wrong?"

"Yes!" I snapped at her.

"I'm so sorry," she didn't look like it with her wicked grin. "English isn't my native tongue. I'm still so easily bamboozled by the language."

I groaned and picked up my sewing cushion and threw it at her in retribution. "What hogwash!"

Jane, my sweet little apprentice, joined in with her laugh. *I had been betrayed!*

I gaped at her. "You too?!"

"I'm sorry, Anne," she at least had the good sense to cringe and look apologetic. "But it is funny."

"It is not!" I grumped.

"Sure, sure," Eather passed me back the cushion and jumped up to sit on the table under the windows, her legs dangling over the edge and swinging as she settled there to see what Jane and I were working on. "Your love life is so serious," she grinned.

I rolled my eyes at her.

"So serious," she continued. "This one was practically your wife! You made it to a full three months. Impressive."

"Only because they hardly saw each other," Jane added on.

Now I used the pillow to smack her up the back of the head. "You need to focus on your work," I chastised. And to Easther, I used my foot to shove her off the table. "And you need to not encourage children to engage in your kind of degenerate filth."

"It's called humour," she rubbed at her ass as she grumbled.

I sneered and lifted the pillow in a threat of more violence. At least this time, she took the warning and went off back to her own projects she was meant to be working on.

Jane still grinned as she started to stich once more, showing that she had been paying attention to her lesson and understood the fundamentals. But also showing that she needed hours of practice to get it right. "I think you should practice with doing a new chemise."

She nodded and scooted across the scarred table top to go and rummage through the linen stash and find something to make into a chemise.

Lucky, the bell on the door in the front of the shop rung out.

I slid off the table and brushed off my skirt as I headed to the curtain that separated the back workroom from the shop front. "Good morning," I smiled as I passed through. "What can I help you with today?"

Mary looked at me, confused. She'd already been serving the new people in.

I still smiled. "Mary, you should take your break now," I suggested to her.

She nodded. "I'm sorry, madams," she spoke to the customers. "But Anne here will be serving you today."

"Oh, that's no problem," one of them announced… and bit her lip as she looked me up and down. "No problem at all." She was attractive. Skin a rich brown. Thick black hair. Cheeky grin.

Oh. I strode across the small space to be at her side immediately. "I'm glad I can be of service," I held her gaze as I said this.

Her companion snorted beside her into her handkerchief.

Yes, we were being obvious. But it was my bloody shop, I think I can allow it to happen. And what was the harm in some flirting?

"My name is Anne. And you might be?"

"Unattached," her friend announced. "She's unattached."

"Hayley!" she hissed.

Mary strode away, pausing to whisper to me. "Behave."

I ignored her. *Why did I employ her? What was the point of employing old friends? Just like the younger generation, they had no respect for you and your position as an employer. Ha! I should go back to working on my own again.*

Less headaches.

Just as Mary was passing through the curtains the bell over the front door rung again.

"Just a moment," I said over my shoulder to the person coming through the door. "I'll get someone to serve you."

A pause. Then. "I can wait."

And my heart stopped.

It was different. Less high pitched, that was to be expected. But it was the same bloody voice and I would recognise it anywhere. I turned to face them and got my first look at my old best friend in what, fourteen years?

"Isa."

She grinned. Crows feet in the corners of her eyes. "Hello Anne." Her gaze darted to the customers behind me and I knew I couldn't indulge any more.

I swallowed. "Please give me a moment." Went to the curtain and hollered. "Mary. I need you out front."

"What happened to my break?" she complained. But came out anyway.

"We have…" I didn't know how to say it. Was Isa a customer? A visitor? An old friend?

But I didn't have to worry. Because Mary's eyes landed on Isa and recognised her immediately and they both exclaimed in shock at seeing each other. Went to talking immediately.

And I wanted nothing more than to join in.

"Sorry about that," I turned back to my current customers I'd poached from Mary. "Now, how may I help you."

As that happened, I switched to professional mode. No more flirting. Much to the disappointed look of the lady before me when she couldn't goad me into it with her co-quettish glances and suggestive double meaning in her words.

At some point, Mary had led Isa out back and I wanted to know immediately what the devil was going on!

"We can do the draping of the pieces right now and set an appointment for you to come back and pick up, say," I looked at the book on the counter and flipped the page over. "End of the week? Are you agreeable with that?"

The women nodded. "That would be lovely."

And then I took them to the little partitioned off space for us to work. "If you wouldn't mind undressing here, while I grab some supplies from the back." And left them to it.

Both wanted new gowns. And so on top of some plain calico fabric, I would be stealing Mary back.

"Mary," I hissed as I went out to the work room. Shocked to find the scene as such; everyone was seated around drinking tea and chatting with Isa. "Oh come on," I nearly snarled.

Easther waved at me. "We're getting to know your old best friend, Anne! She's a great character!"

"Shush you. And stop mucking about," I grabbed the fabric and turned to Mary. "I need you to help me. Both want a gown and it'll be faster if we drape at the same time."

Mary sighed and put aside her tea. "Right. I'll be back," she followed.

Once we were back in the front, I touched her elbow and raised my brows at her.

Mary patted my shoulder, but didn't give me anything else. Just went into the little change room area and started to work.

Twenty minutes later, the two women fully dressed once more, one looking rather desponded at me, they left the shop and I nearly collapsed behind the counter. "Mary!" I hissed.

She rolled her eyes at me. "Come out back and talk to her."

"Not without you telling me what the hell is going on, first. Please," I begged.

Mary scratched at her scalp and considered for a moment. Then marched off.

The bitch!

I followed after her. Or started. I paused at the curtain and just listened to them all laughing and chatting. To the sound of Isa's voice as she spoke.

Lord, I'd missed her.

I pushed through the curtain.

This time Easther had her work on her lap as she chatted away. Waved her hand over it to show it off. "I can multitask," she told me.

"Hmm."

Jane was cutting out her pattern pieces carefully. Pulling a single thread from the fabric to create a shallow line for her to cut along, ensuring she was cutting her fabric perfectly on the grain.

And Mary was actually taking her break and eating.

Isa… well.

Isa stood up from the chair they'd plopped her into and came over to give me a hug. Wrapped me up in her arms and squeezed me tight. "Hello Anne."

I grabbed onto her in return. Rested my chin to her shoulder. "Hello Isa," I whispered back to her.

When she pulled back, I let go. Though I wanted to hold on for longer. Longer than was appropriate. "What are you doing here?" Popped out of my mouth before I could stop it.

Isa laughed and reached into her pocket. "I'm on official business," she said. Then pulled out a piece of paper… a newspaper? And handed it to me.

There, in the black print, was my advert looking for a girl to be a new apprentice mantua maker. I frowned at this.

"I would like to apply," Isa announced.

What?!

I stared. Stupefied. "Excuse me?"

"I would like to apply for the apprenticeship," she told me. But her enthusiasm was dulled. She chewed on her lip. Looked nervous. "If it's open to me," she added on.

My mouth opened and no discernible sound came out. *Isa wanted the apprenticeship?! What?*

Mary coughed. "Maybe you should discuss this in private?" She suggested. "Like your office."

"Yes," burst out of me. And I gestured for Isa to follow as I led her to the cramped space I used for bookkeeping. Closed the door after her. Picked up a stack of paperwork from the one spare chair I had. Laughed. Motioned for her to sit. And finally, sat in my own chair.

Isa didn't look to have the same good humour as before. "You can say no," she said.

I shook my head. "I'm confused."

"About? I thought I was clear."

"Yes and no. You're married."

"Widowed."

"I'm sorry." That sobered me. I wanted to reach out and offer her comfort, but stayed with my hands in my own lap. "Was it recent?"

Isa nodded. "Three months back. He passed. And… I don't know. I wanted to do something and when I saw the advert in the paper and it was to apprentice under you, I thought, why not?"

"Oh."

"But you can tell me no," she protested. "You would probably prefer to give the apprenticeship to someone younger."

"No. I mean, I don't give apprenticeships to just anyone. Age isn't a factor. The same way it is for others."

"Oh?"

I cringed. "It's a little different here. I like to interview and see if someone is the right fit no matter their age or status or anything of the sort. Maybe that's the problem," I pulled a face. "Because that's how I ended up with Easther."

Isa snorted. "She's fun."

"She's a menace."

"But she must do her work well for you not to have fired her."

At that, I did nod in agreeance. Even with her wicked tongue and ability to one up so easily, she was a good worker and I trusted her in the shop.

"Does that mean I should make an appointment for an interview?" Isa directed it back to the topic at hand.

I bit my lip and raised my brows at her. "Are you sure you want to work for me?" That's not what I wanted to say. But I was biting my lip to keep the words from exploding out and hitting her with a barrage of 'yes! It's yours! You can be my apprentice!'

"You employed Mary."

"Ah," I said. Eloquent. "Yes. Mary was a coincidence. And happened a few years back. She's married now. With little ones. But not so little anymore. They're all almost teens. And all boys."

"Good god," Isa's hand came to her chest and eyes widened. "That poor woman."

"Right?" a laugh tinged my voice. "And the only way for her to escape that household was to come and work as a mantua maker. She found my shop. We talked. And then she was my employee. That was about five years ago."

"Was she your first employee?"

"No. I've had my shop for a while. And have had a number come and go. A lot of apprentices. Some older women looking for a wage and not wanting the hassles of having their own business. They've all left for their own reasons. Mary is probably the only one to stay so long. Followed by Easther. Jane is new and just learning the basics." *Wow, I was blabbering.*

Isa nodded along. "Easther and Jane are apprentices?"

"Yep. Jane is fifteen. Easther is twenty and is halfway through her apprenticeship."

"Do they board?"

"No."

"You don't include room and board?" now she looked worried.

"Not for those two," I corrected. "Their families live nearby and so they don't need it." And in some weird desperate moment I made the offer. "But for you, since I'm assuming your husband's family is still all the way up north, I would offer room and board."

Isa's lips started to twitch upwards in the corners. "Does that mean you're offering the apprenticeship?"

I nodded. "Yes. But I do want to see where your skills are at before anything. So, we can adjust things to your current level and you don't start off back at the very beginning."

"That's fair. I have been sewing these last few years. But nowhere near what I should've been doing. I taught my daughter the basics before she went off and into her own apprenticeship."

"You have a daughter?"

"A daughter and a son. There was another little baby…
but I lost it when I was ill and never was able to conceive
another child," she grimaced.

"I'm sorry."

She shrugged. "I got to live and watch my other children grow," her hand drifted to her stomach and paused
there. "It's the way it was meant to be."

"That doesn't make it any easier," I conceded.

"Yes, well. My daughter is thirteen and has been doing
her apprenticeship for one year now. Boarding with the
place. And my son is twelve and he's apprenticing to his
uncle in the family business. He'll be a printer."

"You sound so proud of them already."

"Of course I am! I am proud of my children just for
being." She paused and tilted her head. "Did you ever
marry?"

I shook my head. "No."

"And no children?"

"Also no," I cleared my throat. "As you know, children
require the input of another person."

"That they do," she stared to grin.

"And I don't ever want a man in my life."

"Doesn't it get lonely?" she asked in all seriousness.

I snorted. "Hardly." I flicked my tongue over my lips
and straightened up. "So. You're taking the apprenticeship? It'll include board and wages."

"I'm taking the apprenticeship. Thank you! When do
you want me to start?"

I thought about it for half a second. "As soon as you can. Where are you staying right now?"

"I'm staying at the inn. It would be nice to move into my room immediately."

"Then… this afternoon? Do you want to move in for tonight?" *Oh bugger. I'll need to go and clear out the spare room.*

"This afternoon would be lovely!" she grinned.

There were a few more awkwardly shared details and then she was leaving to go and fetch her things and bring them back. I covered my face with my hands and whined.

"Anne?" Mary prompted.

I huffed. My voice muffled through my palms. "She's the new apprentice."

"That's… nice."

"And she'll be boarding here."

"Boarding?" Easther leapt in. "You never include board."

Mary snickered. "That's because this is Isa. Right Anne?"

I groaned.

"And who is *this* Isa?" Now Easther sounded like she was about to start teasing. "Hmm? Is she the one who got away?"

"Ugh! Shut up! Both of you," I jerked my head out of my hands and glared at them.

Mary's snicker softened and she smiled for real. "It's good to see her again. And it's good that she's coming back to finish her apprenticeship. Two decades later."

"Fourteen years, Mary. Not twenty."

"Where is she boarding?" Jane asked.

And my face burned and I knew they could all see how bright red it had gotten.

"With you?!" Easther cackled. "You're letting her live with you in your flat upstairs? Oh, how scandalous!"

"Hey," I called out over the room. Using my boss voice that shut them up immediately and look at me in blessed silence. "That order needs to be completed today," I pointed at the gown in question. "The pieces for the two new orders need to be cut and organised. And this work space tidied."

"Yes, Anne," they responded.

"If you need me," I grimaced as I added this on. "I'll be upstairs."

A beat passed. "Clearing out the spare room?" Easther asked.

I didn't bother to give her a response. I went stomping up and slumped against my door once I closed it. *What the devil had just happened?!*

"I'm guessing you don't offer board for another reason," Isa added as she looked around the small flat upstairs.

I didn't dignify with a response. *Rude.* This was still my home and a space I was rather comfortable and happy with. Never had any complaints before. But as most of them had come inside for a completely different reason…

"You're over in that room," I pointed across to one of two doors in the space. Doors that were side by side.

She nodded and strode over. After a minute inside she started to talk once more. "I guess it's good for me that I have a room to myself."

"Hmm."

"What are the rules?"

"Rules?" I drifted over to stand in the doorway. This was her room now. I didn't want to traipse inside of it at will without her permission. I'd spent the better part of an hour rushing to clear it out of everything I had stored in it, aired it with the windows cast wide, and cleaned.

I was still sweating from the endeavour.

"You know," she had dropped her bag to the bed and thrown it open. "Curfews and what not."

I snorted. "You're thirty."

She took out her clothes and started to transfer them to the wardrobe. "Yes. But I am your apprentice now."

"Bah," I waved my hand at her and started to walk away.

Her laugh followed me. And it was nice to be hearing it once more.

I went to the small kitchenette, filled the kettle with the water collected that morning from the well, and set it to the stove top.

"What about food?" Isa still talked.

"Are you hungry?" *oh, I hadn't considered that just yet.* I reached into the cupboards to find something to offer her then and there. "I have bread."

"No," she left her room and came over to me. Dropping into the chair at the table and resting her chin onto her hand, propped up by her elbow. "I mean. Board comes with food normally. But do you want me to feed myself?"

I paused. "We can share meals," I said it small. Like I was afraid of actually admitting out loud that I wanted something. That I wanted that.

"We can share meals, but I can buy my own groceries and cook for myself."

"If you want, you can cook for yourself," I managed to get out even and sure sounding. "But board includes food. So, I'll get groceries. If you want to tell me what you want before I go to market, I'll get it."

Why was I being so insistent?

Isa conceded with a laugh. "Okay. Still don't think it's that fair, but okay."

Fair? What needed to be fair?

And then I couldn't be there any longer. I got out a tea cup for Isa to use and made some excuse up. "Kettle is almost boiled. You settle in. I need to go and check on the shop."

"You're not having tea?"

I shook my head and went to the door. "No time. Need to make sure Easther hasn't done the unthinkable."

"The unthinkable?"

"Shut her mouth. I wouldn't want to miss that miracle." I left the flat and hurried down the stairs into the back workroom to find no miracle had happened.

*

Isa joined the team the following day. I assigned her some simple sewing of straight seams on petticoats, inspecting the stitches once she'd done the lengths of either side. Didn't have to tell her to roll the seam allowances over and whip them down to protect the raw edge. As soon as I handed her the paper tape with the measurements of the client nicked into it, she knew what to do and pleated the skirt into the waist measurement. Added it to the waist ties.

I was impressed.

"You didn't forget it all."

Isa chuckled. "Hard to forget. Baby brain made me forget so much. But I would never forget how to sew. It's in my body."

Mary nodded along. "Baby brain," was all she said in agreeance.

"Right," Isa said back to her.

Jane, Easther, and I looked at them with great concern. 'Baby brain?' Easther mouthed out to me.

I shrugged. *Don't ask me. I'm no mother.*

Day after I started Isa on a harder task, still testing her skills. She was set to work on a bodice. Cutting out the pieces in the outer fabric, a lining, and a stiff fabric. Pad stitching the layers together to hold them in place as she worked to bring the whole thing together at the seams. And still finishing off the raw edges to make sure they didn't fray.

And it was in stripe.

Here showed me where her skills sat. And it was not exemplary. "Need help?" I asked her as she stared at the half-finished garment.

"Please," she admitted. "I can't seem to remember what I'm meant to be doing here."

I sat down beside her on the work table and took the project from her. Talked about what she needed to do and showed her as well. Soon, her face shifted and she was taking the project back with excitement in her eyes.

"I get it now!" and was off once more.

I smiled. Happy. Really fucking happy to see her getting lost once more in her work. "Keep it up. You're doing good," I praised. My hand patted her shoulder.

Jane called me over to show her finished chemise off.

*

"Hey, Isa," Easther hissed.

I ignored it. Whatever was happening in the work room wasn't my concern. It was end of month and I was pouring over my books, filling in the blanks I'd been leaving a little too frequent, and then tallying up my expenses and income and… breathing a sigh of relief.

We were not in the red. Thank God! There was a nice little profit and the shop could stay open. Yay!

"Tell us all you know," Easther demanded.

"Mary knew Anne too," Isa replied.

"Not the way you did," Mary added, snidely.

That got my attention. *What on Earth were they gossiping about?*

Isa's giggle was delightful. "I don't know. Anne was like your typical teen. There's not much to say." She paused. "I mean there was this one time when she…"

"When I what?" I startled the four of them all sitting around on the table and working away, but also flapping their gums.

Isa smirked. "When you set fire to that dress."

"She did what?!" Easther tossed her head back and cackled away. Then in Italian, started to say something that I couldn't understand at all.

Mary frowned, then grinned. *Ah shit.* She'd remembered. "I'd forgotten about that."

I glared at Isa, who was looking all too pleased to have revealed something from my past to entertain her audience and vex me, her victim.

"Wasn't that gown the one for a client?" Mary asked Isa.

"It was. But she was so insufferable. Changed her mind over and over about what she wanted. The gown went from a couple of days work to weeks. And then she wanted to change the trimmings, again."

"And that's when Anne lost it?" Jane prompted.

"Completely," Isa continued. "She yelled and carried on and threw the gown into the fire in front of the customer. Mrs Herrick was so pissed."

"How did you not lose your job?" Mary turned to me and queried. "I don't remember it."

"Neither do I," Isa admitted.

"Good," I snapped.

"What a temper," Easther announced. "And you would never guess it by looking at her now."

"Please remember," I stated slowly so they could all keep up. "That I am your employer. And I have no issue with ending your employment effective immediately, if you do not shut up and do the work you're employed to do!" My voice rose at the end.

And though it had been a silly scene only seconds ago, Easther, Jane, and Mary all shut up and ducked their heads. Knowing full well that boss voice was not out all of the time, but when it reared its head, beware.

Isa was the only one looking confused.

But she didn't try to say anything else. Smart. She followed the lead of the others and worked.

*

"Fanny," I greeted. "What a lovely surprise," I said dry and with a straight face.

She grimaced. "Trust me, I am not happy to see you either, Anne."

"You're so sweet. Where's your usual helper? She's so much more delightful to deal with." I leaned against the front counter as she came into the shop and dropped packages out in front of me.

Her eyes dropped down briefly and looked at my breasts. Before snapping back to my face. "She's no longer my employee," she said. Sour.

"Oh? Did she wise up and leave you?" I snapped back, catty and not caring that this was another business owner I had to deal with.

"Yes. And with half my bloody clientele," she sniped. "But since she didn't take you, I guess that meant she didn't like you half as much as you liked her."

Shit. I blinked at that, a little stupefied. "Sorry about that hit to your ego," I said with full sympathy. "Things must be tough."

Fanny sniffed and raised her nose to the air. *There it was. Her bitchiness.* "Hardly. My business has an outstanding reputation built on years. Those fools will realise their mistake once she messes up order after order on them."

"Or they'll accept accidents. Especially when she had that sweet face… unlike you," I couldn't resist. Had to jab away at this woman. She had a beautiful face and knew it. But a pretty face didn't hide a shitty personality.

She rolled her eyes. "You're such a…"

"Ahahh," I grinned as I waggled my finger in her face. "I'm a customer to your humble. Little. Business."

Lord, why was it so nice to pull this woman back down to Earth every time we crossed paths? Like, very enjoyable. Almost, orgasmic to see her face begin to turn red and she was forced to have to deal with me. And especially now that I was one of her remaining loyal clients.

Then again, she always had the best trim and a wide variety to choose from. Not like I could go elsewhere.

"Still a bitch," she hissed under her breath. As if she couldn't help herself.

And that made me laugh. "You like my money."

"It's the only thing I can accept from you."

"It's the only thing I will ever offer you."

We concluded our business. I checked off the contents of each packet against what I'd ordered. Paid the account for the month. Sent her away without care.

And turned to hand this all off to Easther to organise in the back of the shop.

Isa gaped at me. "That's how you talk to you milliner?"

I ignored and went back out to the front counter, taking some work with me to finish off while I sat there and waited for the one o'clock appointment.

"Of course that's how they talk," Easther told her. And I could hear every word. "But it would be preferable for them to just shut up and make out already!" she shouted the last part.

I parted the curtain to glare at her. "Refrain from yelling that when we are expecting customers," I warned her.

"So, you do want to make out with Fanny," she said it so self-assured.

"I'm docking your pay," I dropped the curtain and went back to work.

"End our suffering!" Easther complained. "Please! Fighting is just foreplay! All of this sexual tension each time you two run into each other is…" the bell on the door rang out and Easther shut up.

"Good afternoon," I sat aside the sewing and stood up to greet the customer. "You're right on time."

*

"You like women?" Isa asked over dinner.

Unfortunately, while I was drinking wine. I inhaled it instead of swallowing and coughed and spluttered to clear it out. "Excuse me?"

Isa waited for me to grab the corner of my apron and lift it to my face. "Over men?" she continued.

I picked up the fork and stabbed into the Shepards pie in my bowl. "As in what way?" Oh, I knew what she was meaning. But I never expected to have to have the conversation with her over dinner on a weeknight.

"Well, you never married."

Obvious.

"And when we went to dances, you hated it when boys would approach us."

Obvious.

"And Easther and Mary said that you had… had lovers who were women."

I'm firing them. They're not even getting their last pay. Nope. I'm keeping it all as compensation for this suffering they were now forcing upon me. Their families starving and being kicked out of their homes and living in the streets would never compare to how I suffered right then and there.

"If you know all of that, then why ask?" I shovelled food into my mouth.

Isa shrugged. Her fingers twirled the fork, pushing her food around in her bowl in a way that any mother would scold their child for.

"Are you going to answer?" she still pushed.

I grimaced. "What is the question?"

"Do you…" she paused as she thought about it. "Do you have a preference for your lovers? Gender." She tacked on the last word.

"Um…" *oh fuck. Sweet baby Jesus. What am I meant to do here?!* I cleared my throat. "I do." *Forget it. I want to escape, I do not wish to be having this conversation at all with my old best friend. That very same best friend I had been in love with. Who had been very flirty and familiar with me when we'd been sixteen.*

But then went and fell in love with a man!

I do not want to be having this discussion or admitting to things or having her put two and two together and coming out with a hundred different possibilities. Was it too late to say I was ill and didn't want dinner?

"Anne," she laughed. And it was light and warm. "Don't look so panicked. I'm just asking about your love life."

That's the problem. "It's not necessarily something I like to discuss."

"Because it's a mess?"

I gaped at her.

She giggled. "Easther's words. Well, she used other words. But they were not so kind."

"Ohhhhhhhh," I started to devise all of the awful things I was going to be assigning to her tomorrow. All of the reorganising and cleaning and the fiddly trims to be added to the bottoms of that gown that we were finishing up. Oh, and stern words about her behaviour. *Brat.*

Isa laughed. "So you like women?"

"Yes," I admitted.

"Have you ever… tried with a man?"

I scoffed. "No. Never. No thank you."

"Then how do you know that you like women?"

I stared at her. What a daft question to ask. "How did you know you liked men? It's not like you tried with a woman before getting married." *Oh, that sounded way more like an accusation.*

Isa paused. "I mean."

"What?" I gaped at her. "When?!" *And with whom?*

She shook her head. "I never tried. Only, considered it."

"With whom?" I still demanded.

And then she was fixing me with that 'you're stupid' look. "Who do you think?"

Still, don't know. I threw my hands up and flapped my lips in utter confusion. Unable to ask again as to who it was that had caught her eye.

It stung. The thought of her having been interested in a woman before getting married. Thinking about it… about me being in love with her… and her being curious for another woman.

She rolled her eyes this time. "We use to flirt all of the time, Anne. Us." She added on to confirm it, her finger pointing to her chest and then to… me.

And then I stared at her with eyes so wide and no other thoughts.

"Who else was I spending all of my time with before meeting my husband? Who else was I so close to? Hmm?"

I had no idea.

"But we were sixteen. And bad at flirting," she continued.

"It had been intentional?!" blurted out of my mouth.

She leaned back in her chair and just laughed. Laughed so hard she had to cover her mouth with both hands and nod her response to my outburst.

"I never knew," I admitted. Slumping a little. And wondering about what could've been… and the way it would've hurt more if we had been lovers when she had married. How that would've destroyed our friendship. How we wouldn't be sitting here across from each other if it had happened.

Isa must've laughed so hard that she was swiping her wrist under her eyes. She started to reach over and with her thumb, brushed it firmly over the corner of my mouth. "You're making a mess," she said and sat back in her seat. Taking up her fork once more.

Gobsmacked.

Panicked.

Unsure of every fucking thing.

"So," Isa began. "What's the truth and what has Easther exaggerated?"

I huffed. "Unfortunately, Eather doesn't exaggerate. She says a lot of things, but never not the truth. A good little Italian Catholic girl she's turned out to be. Her mother is so proud." And though my words stank of sarcasm, they too were honest and true.

Isa blinked at me in shock. "Really? So you and… an actual lady had a thing going on?"

"Hmm? Lizzie?" then slapped my hand over my mouth as I realised I'd confirmed it.

Isa's jaw dropped. "No," she said in disbelief. "I thought for sure Easther had been joking about that one."

"She's going to be unemployed," I informed her.

"How did you and a lady of high standing… you know?" she used her hand to wave in the air in this little roll. As if that was descriptive.

I shook my head. "I do not kiss and tell."

"Why not?"

"Because that's improper," I then turned it around on her. "Would you tell me all of the details about you and your husband?"

"Probably," she admitted.

"Why?" Just the thought of knowing something about him made me ill. I looked at dinner and considered not finishing it for fear of reseeing it again if Isa decided she wanted to talk about the good days with him.

But my face must've spoken of the horrors I was thinking and she spared me with laughing instead. "I won't, I won't. I promise."

"Please, keep that to yourself," I almost demanded she pinky swear it. For fear was awful as a companion with nausea.

"You have no desire for men?" she asked again.

"None," I told her firmly. "I have never liked them and I think I will continue until death to never want them."

"Hmm," she hummed to herself.

"Why do you ask?" I finally ate another bite. This time, it was almost cold.

She shrugged. "Just comparing," and drank from her wine.

"Anne?"

"Hmm?"

"What do you look for in a lover?"

Every other thought evaporated and I was dumb. Didn't know a thing as I sat there staring at the work I'd been doing. At the garment I'd been constructing out of expensive silk, only that I knew, I didn't have a clue how it had been made thus far or how to finish it off.

"Pardon?" Finally came out of my mouth. A lot louder than her words.

Isa didn't stop her stitches. Nor did she look up at me to study my reaction. She just sat on the table and worked away. And her words were soft, so it was not clearly overheard by the rest in the room, a private conversation.

Except for my outburst.

Easther looked up. Eager. "What are you begging to be pardoned for, Anne? What did you do?"

I don't know! I am dumb.

Isa giggled and slipped in. "She's panicking."

"Over?" Easther prompted. Pushed.

"A question I asked."

Finally, my brain caught up. "Stop gossiping. I'm right in front of you," I gave her a glare.

Still, she worked away and giggled some more.

Lord, that laugh.

Later that evening, there was no escaping the question again. "What do you look for in your lovers?" She asked this as we ate.

I grimaced. "I don't know." *I did know.* It had been pointed out to me that I had certain preferences. And I was very aware as to where they'd come from.

"Does she have to be pretty?" Isa insisted.

Yes. "Why are you asking this?"

"I want to know."

"Why? Are you planning on matchmaking?" That made me feel... wrong. I wasn't in love with this Isa that I was getting to know now. I had loved the sixteen-year-old Isa, had mourned the loss of her when she had married someone else. But I wasn't in love with her now.

Except... I felt something for her. More than that warm feeling of friendship. As if I was having the start of a crush again.

Or maybe it was just Isa and this was how I normally felt for her. That it was something more than friendship. Maybe it would never progress to something else. Maybe this was my feelings for a best friend. Maybe I didn't know nor wanted to understand all of this and just wanted to enjoy living and working with her for as long as I had her.

After all, she would be leaving again once she completed her apprenticeship.

She hadn't said it, but most left. Most went out on their own or went and got pregnant and took time away but never returned.

Isa would leave me. Again. And that was fine. It was expected.

"Would you like me to pick out a lover for you?" she queried.

"No thanks," I huffed. "I don't trust your judgement."

"Why not?"

"I saw what you married."

She gaped at me. Unable to make a comeback to that.

I grinned. Felt triumphant! That was a point to me. And I was spending too much time around Easther and her fast wit.

*

But it wasn't just her questions. Isa started to... be more friendly in her touch.

Not unwelcomed! Not at all.

But it was something that she'd refrained from doing since she'd started working for me. Unless it was the usual thing of hands touching when something was being passed to one another, there was nothing.

Now, it was intentional.

Her hand on my lower back as she asked me to step aside. Hands on my waist as she looked over my shoulder, and then her chin to that shoulder.

"I'm exhausted," Isa announced. To demonstrate just how tired she was, she flopped over my back, arms coming around to hug me, and her face buried into the crook of my neck.

We were in the fucking front of the store.

I elbowed her. "A customer could see you doing this," I hissed. The shop was empty. But still. "Be professional."

She whined and clung tighter still. Pressed her face firmly against my neck and... *did she?!*

"Did you just lick me?!" I struggled to break free of her.

But she squeezed and held tight. "Noooooo," she complained.

"Quit slobbering on me," I ordered.

"Not slobbering."

"You just licked me!" Could feel that moisture clinging to my neck. *Ugh! Gross.*

With a heavy sigh she released and wandered off. "I am not a dog," Isa stated. Firm.

"Then don't go around licking people!" I threw back at her, fishing out a handkerchief from my pocket and wiping at the area she'd marked.

"Ugh," she grumped. "You're so oblivious."

"What?!"

Only she'd slipped back through the curtain and a customer came in through the front door, setting off the bells overhead.

Other than the licking incident that shall never be spoken of again… I was enjoying this level of affection. I'd missed it. And I craved more.

"Isa," I beckoned her over the next day. A basket over my arm and cloak over my shoulders. "Want to come to the market with me?"

It was early. The shop was open, but Mary could hold the fort while I was out, and once Easther and Jane arrived, she'd be fine. And I didn't see any harm in taking Isa away from her work for the morning.

She looked up excited. "Sure. Let me get ready," and bounded off with way too much energy for so early.

Mary snickered.

"What?" I demanded of her.

She was cutting out fabric. Long straight lines. And instead of being careful, she was nicking the edge and gripping the two sides into her fists and ripping them apart. Loud *sqreeeach* sounds in the quiet.

It sure as hell was faster than pulling a single weft and cutting into the ditch left behind ever so meticulous with each *snip snip*.

"What?" I demanded again as she only raised a brow at me.

"Have fun on your little date," she commented.

"It's not like that. We're going to the market for food," I countered.

"Anne, you're not that dense. And Isa isn't that subtle."

Isa came back down the stairs, her cheeks flushed from her rush up and down them, hair starting to loosen from her pins and escape her white cap, and cloak swirling around her. *Beautiful.*

My mouth was… open. Jaw hanging. When I realised, I snapped it shut and shook my head to clear it. "Let's go," I hustled to the door.

Isa followed.

When we were outside and she was by my side, I made my move. Took a deep breath. And looped my arm through hers.

She bent her arm to give me something more to hook and hold onto.

And then…

With her free hand, she cupped my hand on her arm and fucking rubbed her fingers over it. Soothing.

Oh Hell!

Good Lord!

Isa giggled and pointed something out, her hand leaving mine for a moment but coming back immediately.

We shopped. I barely paid attention. Isa seemed to realise it and took over, taking my purse and going full house wife. And I was pulled around by her to simply carry what she'd purchased in my little basket.

On the way back to the shop, she leaned in close and whispered into my ear. She'd been doing that all morning. Coming in close to share things. 'Look at that dress.' 'Do you remember?' 'I forgot to tell you.'

But what came out of her mouth now as we approached the shop, approached our home… *Lord have mercy.*

"Anne," she slowed her steps. Dragging her feet a little and forcing me to match. "I have a favour to ask."

"What is it?" Already feeling like I would agree to it, no matter what it was. It was Isa. I'd been her maid of honour for her wedding as she married another. I'd agreed to giving her an apprenticeship, with board. I'm not sure what she could ask for that I could refuse her.

"Um," she dipped her head.

Was she blushing?

Now, we'd stopped on the street. Ten steps away from the front of the shop. I could see my sign hanging above the door, could read my name there and see the symbol of the spool of thread and needle I used to announce my wares and services to those who could not read letters. Could see in through the window. Spot Mary talking with a customer.

But I was focussed on the fidgeting of Isa. Her hand still over mine played with my fingers. Her head was down.

"What's wrong?" I asked. Resisting the urge to cup her cheek and make her look at me, since my other arm was weighed down by the basket. "Are you in trouble?"

She shook her head and snapped it up. "No. I'm in no trouble."

It wasn't easier with her looking at me. But at least it was not so scary now. "Then what?"

She grimaced. Eyes flicked away and then back to me, then away again. She wet her lips with the tip of her tongue. "I want you to make love to me… with me," Isa corrected.

My heart dropped from my chest. It kept falling.

What had she asked?

Why had she asked that?

"Huh?" came out oh so eloquently.

"If you want to," she continued on. "I'm not going to force you to do anything. It's just… yeah."

"You…" I tried to start. Tried my best to force words out of my mouth and to ask for clarification. Maybe she didn't mean what I was immediately allowing my brain to jump to. Maybe she was asking for something else. Maybe I misheard. Maybe I was insane and should be locked up.

"You don't…" I tried again. "Mean… Do you mean…" *Oh for the love of God, woman! Get your shit together already.*

Isa nodded. "I do mean it. I mean every word of it, Anne. I want you to show me how two women have sex."

Oh.

No.

Wait.

What? How? Like as in how two women did it? Like she was curious and that was it?

Like she just saw me as a convenient teacher because I was one of the first women she knew who had been with other women? Was that what she meant?

"Isa," I hissed. Pissed off was an understatement. What the devil was I to Isa? "If you're curious, go and read about it," I snapped at her.

"There are books?" she was shocked.

"I am not sleeping with you just to sate your bloody curiosity." I nearly stormed off, except for the grip she had on my arm. "Let me go."

"No," she shook her head. "You've got this wrong, Anne."

"Do I?"

"Yes," she hissed. "I did not mean to word it in a way to imply you are to perform for me. I adore you, Anne. You are my precious friend."

Under that praise, my anger faded. And hurt stayed. "Then what are you talking about?"

"I trust you."

Oh damnation.

"And if you too find me attractive," she continued. "I'd hoped you would… educate me… and allow me to give you pleasure back."

My mind went blank.

…

…

…

I took the basket off my arm and mechanically handed it to Isa who was so dark in the face with her blush and watching me with huge eyes. She accepted the offering.

"Anne?"

I waved her off. "I um, need to go to the… uh… need to go to the market."

"Anne, we'd just been there," she lifted the basket now in her hands.

Didn't matter. "Forgot something." And then I was steps away from her. I turned my back to her and hurried.

"I have your purse," she called after me.

But I didn't stop.

Didn't slow.

Just hauled my ass out of there as fast as my feet could carry me down the street and away from her. Where I was heading, I had no clue. Didn't care at all.

But I couldn't go into the shop and act all normal with everyone. One wrong comment from Easther and I was going to lose it. One teasing remark… *oh hell.*

Isa had asked me to take her to bed.

Had said she'd wanted to give me pleasure in return.

Isa had said this. All with a seriousness that I could never understand for such a topic, on the street! She discussed it like it was some common occurrence for idle chatter.

And I was back to the horrible realisation that I was… *oh bloody hell.* Lord give me the strength to process this. Because surely I was not… but yes. My answer was going to be yes.

So, I walked. Heels clicking on the cobble. Letting my body react and get me out of the way of other pedestrians. Turned random corners and took streets I rarely used.

Hoping that my mind would supply me with a different answer. That I would be able to rationalise all of the ways that this was going to mess things up between us and come to the conclusion that a refusal was best. That we shouldn't go to bed together. That it may be a little awkward now, but hey, that's okay.

Better than how it will hurt in the end.

Preferrable.

Awkward for having to refuse a request like this and taking a few days for it to be forgotten and replaced by other things, was preferrable.

Because…

Because…

I swallowed hard. Because if I got to be like that with Isa, I don't think I could survive her leaving me again.

Oh, bah! How pathetic was I?! Seriously? Couldn't survive without her? Hardly. I was a grown woman with more things in my life than just a lover to dedicate all of my time and energy. I had ambitions and friends and a business I was proud to call my own.

My heart had been broken a few times over the years. But it never stopped me from living.

And the same will be true here.

It wasn't like I was in love with Isa as she was now.

So, I marched back to the shop. Entered through the front door. Ignored Mary who looked up in surprise from helping a customer select fabric from the samples. Pushed through the curtain.

Isa jerked her head up from where it had been down and dejected. There was a definite pout on her lips. And tears in her eyes.

Both Jane and Easther were on either side of her consoling her.

"Yes." Blurted out of my mouth. No self-control at all. Isa blinked at me.

My announcement made, I nodded to her and turned on my heel. Following me out was her giggle and Easther yelling. "Yes what?"

I stormed out of the shop again to wander the streets for an undetermined time.

Sweet merciful Jesus, what had I just agreed to?!

*

End of the day. I was so worked up. Why had she asked me in the morning? And why had I arrived at my decision so early? Because now I've suffered hours of knowing that I had agreed to taking her to bed and showing her how two women made love to each other, and then worrying about showing her how to women made love to each other.

Isa had never been with a woman.

She claimed to have been curious about it when we were apprentices, before she got married.

Oh God, she'd been with a man. What if I couldn't compare at all to her past experience? What if I was not only no better than but worse than a man at giving her pleasure?

Pull yourself together! You've had other lovers who had more experience and multiple types of partners.

But they had not been Isa.

And I'm starting to realise why I didn't like to mix lust with friendship. This is too fucking stressful.

"You can still say no," Isa reminded me. Grounded me then and there with her voice suddenly filling the room. My room.

Since when had we moved into here?

I shook my head to clear it. "Sorry. I'm just… damn it. I've been obsessing over this all day. You have no idea how you tortured me with this," I admitted to her.

She gave a short little laugh. "I'm talented like that." Paused. "And you're not the only one."

As if it had been her bed and not mine, she dropped to sit on the edge and patted the space beside her. Wary, I took it. Felt my body sway, wanting to lean into her the way it had done so many times so many years ago.

"I'm nervous," she admitted.

"That makes two of us."

"But you're the one who knows what they're doing here."

"And? This is different. It's always different."

"How so?"

I took a moment to really consider it. "Each person is different. They all have different experiences and preferences. Some like one thing but another hates it and will never do it."

"I've only ever been with my husband," she admitted.

I tried not to grimace at that. Her having history before me wasn't a problem. But because it was *him* and it had happened when I had been in love with her, that meant it was still something that stung. A reminder I didn't enjoy.

We sat in silence for a moment.

"Are we..." she started.

I swallowed. "I'm willing. If you're still willing."

"I'm willing."

"Then," I breathed out and straightened my back. "We should start."

"Okay."

More of an awkward pause.

That was broken when both of us dissolved into giggles. Giggling so hard, we collapsed into one another and fell backwards to the bed together. "What are we doing?" I asked her.

"I don't know," she buried her giggling face into my neck.

"Ah! Don't slobber on me again."

"I didn't before," she tried to grumble, but the effect was lost under the laugh.

"Then what was it?"

She groaned. "A kiss."

Oh. "Oh…" I reached up and brushed her hair from her face.

She removed herself from my neck and looked up at me.

And I kissed her. Soft and sweet. She pushed up and kissed me back. Her lips moving under mine with a practised ease. We shifted around until we found a spot that felt comfortable, where we were able to maintain our kiss indefinitely if we wished. Me on my back. Isa draped half over my body. Arms wrapped around her waist.

A hand trailing down and up her hip.

And then her thigh.

And then she hiked her thigh up and over my hip and *Lord.*

One thing flowed into the next. The temperature went high and I was itching to get us both undressed. Hot and heavy. The sound of our lips smacking and the slight creaking of the bed as we rocked unconsciously into each other.

I broke the kiss. Panting into her open mouth as she panted into mine. "Isa," I forced out. "Are you sure?"

She had her forehead pressed to mine. Nodded against it. "Very. Please, Anne."

I nodded back to her and then it was a mess of fumbling. Of stripping off while we were still a tangle on the bed. Laughing as we struggled. Threw off offending items of clothing.

I stopped to worship the skin she revealed. The swell of her breasts over her stays with my lips. Loved that she clung to my head and pressed me closer still.

Then the stays were unlaced and off. Chemise pulled over head.

Naked.

We were bare to each other.

"Isa," I grabbed her attention back as her lips started to trail up and down my throat, nipping the sensitive skin in some places and making me gasp. "Lie back," I ordered her.

She did.

I came to my knees and looked down at her, laid out. Hair spreading over the sheets in a mess. Chest rising fast with each gasp of air. And her thighs parting to either side of me.

She bit her bottom lip as she watched me lower down.

I laid on my belly. Got her to drape her legs over my shoulders. Used my fingers to part her and placed my mouth over her. I took my time to tease. To have my spit pool and coat her.

Then, as if it was a normal kiss, I started to make out with her clitoris. Lips soft. Tongue dragging and then flicking. Wet and filthy sounds filled the air.

And then…

"Anne," Isa gasped and grabbed my hair.

There. That was the motion. I repeated it over and over. Letting her tell me when it was too much or too little with her hums and grip in my hair and hips pushing up into my mouth or retreating back into the bedding to get away. I did what she told me to do.

And was rewarded with her screams as she came.

Lost some hair in the process, I'm sure. But worth it.

Her thighs gripped my head. Squished my cheeks together. Lord, I loved it.

Slowly, I disentangled from her and moved up to lie beside her.

Not even waiting, she threw her arms around me and kissed. Grimaced. "Is that what I taste like?" she asked.

I nodded.

She kissed again. Must've not worried her as she kept kissing me and tasting herself.

I ached. Whined. "Isa," pulled her in tight.

"Want me to…" she started to pull back.

I shook my head. "No. Just. Do this," and I didn't have the words to explain. I moved her leg, pushed it between my own and pressed against it. The friction of my clit being dragged over her thigh. My hips rocked at the pace I liked.

She cupped my breast and fondled.

I came. Head buried into her hair. Hips slowing in their rocking. Until I stopped and lifted up to look at her.

"Is that how?" she was still panting.

I snorted. "Only two ways of doing it… want to see another three ways?"

Her eyes widened. "More? Right now?"

“Yeah. More. Right now. If you’re ready to go again.”
“Yes! God, yes please!”

I'm slow to wake the next morning. Happy. Warm. Weighted. I stretched out a bit in bed, my arms going overhead to the headboard, toes pointing. "Hmmmm," I pushed just a little harder for that stretch then released with a grunt.

Arms came back down and wrapped around…

"Hmm?" I looked. Dark hair. A mess of dark hair.

There was a woman in my bed. It takes a full moment for me to remember the night before. To stop and think about what the hell happened and how Isa had curled up in my arms and stayed. *Oh my!* Isa had spent the night in my bed!

Isa and I had slept together.

We'd… all night. Not all night, that's an exaggeration. But for a good few hours we'd touched each other.

I had tasted her!

Holy Mother of God!

Isa lifted her head and looked at me with the same sleepy expression she'd throw at me as apprentices, only she'd been in her own bed and looking over at me in mine. *It was so cute!* Her hair rumpled. Cheeks with the imprint of creases from the sheets. Soft. And then she tilted her lips upwards. "Morning," she moved from my chest and kissed me.

"Morning," I replied. Kissed her back.

No tension at all in Isa as she laid there. She hummed. Content.

I sucked her bottom lip into my mouth. Rubbed my tongue over it. Her leg hitched up. I caught it with my hand on instinct and hooked it over my hip. Trailed my hand along her thigh…

It wasn't something that either of us was planning in the morning. But one moment flowed into the next and she gasped into my mouth. Rocked herself on my fingers. Then I was rocking on her fingers.

Not in perfect timing to each other. But it was close. Then we were close to reaching our peaks. Movements getting erratic. Hurried. More gasping for air.

I came first.

She followed.

A lovely way to wake up in the morning.

*

The weeks that followed were strange. For no other reason than we simply became… lovers. I had rather assumed this had been a one-time thing. That once Isa had her first experience with a woman that she would not do it again with me unless the mood struck.

I was wrong.

That first evening after work. As we laughed and chatted and got ready for bed… she followed me to my room.

I didn't question it. Accepted it immediately.

Wondered briefly if she was just giddy from what we'd done the night before and wanted more of that same feeling.

"I want to," she told me between kisses. "With my mouth." *Kiss.* "For you."

I groaned and couldn't deny her. *Dear God.* I couldn't deny her anything, especially when she sounded so desperate. I nodded. "Please."

"Tell me what to do. I've never done it before."

Obvious.

"Undress me," I ordered.

She kept my eye contact as she did so. Discarded my outer layers to the floor without a care. As she unlaced my stays… "Hmmm," I moaned.

She laughed. "You always prefer to be out of these." Helped me out of them completely.

I reached over and traced my fingers over the swell of her breasts, still confined and pushed up and together by her stays. "They're necessary," I conceded. "But it's nice to be out of it at the end of the day."

"There are other options to them," she dropped it to the floor. "Softer. Less rigid things you could wear instead."

"Oh?" I knew of them. Of course. But… I don't know. Never got around to trying the alternatives to my stays. And what I wore showed people what I could make for them. So, I had to wear what they wanted to see with the appropriate underpinnings.

Isa didn't answer. Was distracted.

Her hands came up and cupped my breasts through the chemise. Played with them to her own fascination. Thumbed my nipples through the fabric until they stood to attention for her.

I undressed her with the same care. Discarding everything in the way until she was the same as I and then I took a step further and got rid of that last piece of linen hiding her body. Stroked my hands over the swell of her hips. Traced stretch marks. Liked that I could take a firm grip and she would gasp and lean into it.

Shit.

"Anne," she whined. One of her hands went down and cupped my sex through the chemise.

"Shit," I repeated.

Reminded me of what she'd requested. Got myself naked and onto the bed. Directed her to be on her stomach. Then paused. "There's another way," I told her.

"Huh?"

"Lay on your back here," and rearranged so she was down and I straddled her head.

She stared up at me in wild fascination. "Like this?"

I nodded.

"You're going to sit on me," she giggled at it.

I chuffed. "Something like that."

Experimentally, she flicked her tongue out and caught my clitoris with it's tip. "Sit on my face, Anne," she demanded.

After that night, the next one wasn't a shock to have Isa follow me to my room. For us to make each other breathless and sweaty and greedy for more. Another night followed. Another. A week. Two.

Always with us together.

Sometimes soft and sleepy, barely awake as we skimmed each other's bodies with tired fingers. Other times hard and demanding. Hurried. Desperate to get to each other and bring pleasure and feel it.

Isa went to her room for something one evening. I wondered briefly if she was going to sleep alone…

But I wasn't going to intrude on her. Sometimes people needed that time and space to themselves. I knew that. I enjoyed it. But I had my office to lock myself into during the day and escape Easther. There were times, I would sit in there and work away all day and not talk to anyone.

Which was one of the reasons why I never fired an employee.

Mary was my godsend. My absolute saint! She could run the shop alone and handle the apprentices with ease. She didn't need me there except to pay her wages at the end of the day.

Easther was excellent with customers and would make a fine mantua maker in the end.

And Jane would grow into herself. It was unclear as to who she was right now, being fifteen and trying things out for the first time.

I had my space.

Maybe Isa needed hers.

I went to my room and started to get ready for bed.

But Isa hadn't given any indication that she was needing space over dinner. The opposite, actually. Considering how she found some excuse to touch me in a way. Be it her knees pressed to mine. Holding hands on the table top. Cleaning up a mess of crumbs from my face with her smiling at me.

I was letting my hair down when she came back to the room, grinning like a fool that was up to something.

And my chest fluttered. She wasn't upset with me. "What?" I said, curious yet cautious.

She widened her eyes in a poor attempt to be innocent looking. "I have a… an exchanging of wisdoms."

"A what now?" I rapidly blinked at her in utter confusion. What could she possibly be wanting to educate me with?

Her sly smile grew and she jerked her chin to the bed. "Sit."

I did as she instructed.

"Hold out your hand."

"Is it going to bite me?" I asked.

"Do you want it to?"

"What kind of response is that?!" I yelped and pulled my hand back to the safety of my chest.

Still, she insisted. "Hold out your hand."

"Ugh," I did.

"Close your eyes."

"No. Just… show me."

Rolling her own eyes, she withdrew the item from behind her back. Laid it upon my hand. And waited.

"Oh," I said with interest. My fingers curled around its round shape to hold in place.

"Ever used one?" Isa asked.

I shook my head. "An old lover had a collection of them, but I never trusted her enough to… allow her to use one on me."

Isa cocked her brow. "Never thought of getting your own to use alone?"

My face started to burn. I shook my head.

"Do you…"

I nodded. "Please," I swallowed.

Isa stepped in close. Her hand cupped my jaw, thumb tracing my lips. "You trust me?" She asked.

"It's you Isa. I trust you," I told her the truth.

She bent down and kissed me while taking the dildo from my hands as she did. "Then I need you naked and on the bed for me."

Yes ma'am! I did as she instructed. Watched as she too stripped and climbed onto the mattress beside me. She placed the head of the toy into her mouth and sucked it, leaving it shiny and wet as she pulled it out.

"Where did you get this?" I asked. Wanting to say something and not focus on the growing… nerves. That thing was designed to fuck someone. The same way a man fucked.

Isa's mouth was a distraction. It was red and open and every time she dipped the dildo back in she hummed around it. Then she was pressing it to my mouth. I opened. It wasn't a normal thing for me to be excited over having something she'd been sucking on in my mouth… or the realisation that she'd used this on herself and now it was in me. And would be inside of me proper in moments.

Lord.

Why was that so appealing?

Why was the thought alone making me fidget and ache.

She smiled. "I got this from a market stall. Being sold in broad daylight. Wooden cocks all over the place."

I laughed around the head of it.

She bit her lip. "I liked the size of this one. It's a nice shape and width." Isa continued.

Taking it once more back into her hands, she guided it down my body, pressed it between my lips. Circled my clitoris. Dipped lower.

"Are you sure? You don't have to," she asked. Her head was against my neck. She'd slipped down lower on the bed to give her better access. A better angle to touch me with the toy.

I gripped her hair in one hand and the sheet in the other. "I'm sure. Fuck me, Isa. Please."

She did.

*

My monthly bleed arrived. Along with cramps that had me curling up and wanting to die. I was in my office when I first noticed the discomfort. Had written it off as maybe needing the chamber pot sooner rather than later.

But then, it was that horrible pain that radiated from my abdomen and lower back.

Yep. It was that time of the month.

I stumbled out of the office and waved to the others as I headed to the stairs, hand cradling my belly as I went.

Inside my room I rummaged for a liner. Grimaced as I realised that I had been too late and blood was already on my petticoat.

Great. I grumbled as I took it off. Then decided that I would get down to more comfortable layers and curl up and feel like I was dying for a while.

Liner in place, stays off, I went to the kitchen to stoke the fire in the stove.

"Anne?" Isa came in through the door.

I waved to her. "Hey," I forced out through my pinched lips.

"What's the matter? Are you ill?"

"Bleeding. The usual."

She nodded in understanding. Took in my state of undress and how I moved the skillet to the stove top. "Go lie down," she came and took over. Taking the small stones I was about to toss into the pan and heat. "I'll get this prepared for you."

"I can do it," I protested.

"Let me," she was more gentle.

I nodded and went to bed. Curled up as best I could with my pillow in my grip and rode the pain.

Isa came in with the stones wrapped in a cloth bundle and handed them to me to position. I laid them on my stomach. She then offered me a tea. "It's got something in it," she told me.

"Something good?" I sighed as the heat pushed into my muscles and forced them to relax. But I also started to feel sweat forming on my skin.

"To help with the pain," she nodded. "Nothing too strong."

"Strong isn't a problem," I said and sat up enough to drink. "If it could knock me out and I didn't have to be awake for this, I would not complain."

She chuckled. "Want some laundrum instead?"

I shook my head. "Save it for when it's really bad."

She nodded.

"What was in that tea?" I had tasted it but still wanted her to speak to me. Even for a moment longer before she had to go back down and work.

She sat on the bed and started to stroke my hair. "Whiskey."

"Knew it," I smiled at her.

"Then why ask?"

I shrugged.

Moments passed with her sitting there. We chatted about nonsense. Until she stopped stroking my hair. "I'll be back," she said and stood.

I waved at her. Not wanting her to leave, but knowing that she did have to go back and help the others. Especially if I was unable to do so. Not that Mary would be surprised. Nor would it be a surprise for any of them to ask for leave or need a chance to do something easier for the day because of their own issues.

Lord, I loved my own business. Dictating what was acceptable and not having to adhere anymore to someone else's horseshit.

And that thought took me to a memory of working for someone else. After Mrs Herrick but before having my own shop. And how they didn't care. Even though they themselves were women and knew and could understand. They just didn't. A mother couldn't ask for time off to care for a sick child. Menstruation was never an excuse for being 'lazy.'

Ha!

Mrs Herrick taught me my trade.

That place, that shall remain nameless, taught me my values.

And here I was, living out my values.

And sweating. Goodness, Isa had heated the stones up like crazy. The whiskey wasn't helping either. I kicked at the blankets. Rolled and rocked. Trying to soothe. Trying to find some bit of comfort.

Needed a distraction.

Considered going to the window and looking out. People watch as they went about their day. But that was on the other side of the room and not a place I could sit comfortably.

I huffed.

Uncomfortable still. Edgy.

Maybe I should move to the small sitting room and find a book to read. Or do some knitting. The basket was in there.

But still, the act of getting up and doing that was not an option. So, I stewed.

Until Isa returned. She came back up sooner than expected. I thought the end of the day, once everything was closed up. Not an hour later she was back and taking my little package of stones and tea cup away, returning them reheated and refilled.

"Are you bored?" she asked.

I nodded. Feeling sooky and wanting her to stay and keep me company.

"Want a book?"

I nodded again.

She fetched me some. Left. Returned an hour later.

Over and over until it was the end of the day and I was feeling better. Less like I was dying and was able to move to the kitchen table for food.

"Thank you for today," I told her.

She shook her head. "That was no problem." Something on her face said she was ready to do it all again next month.

I ignored that. Probably reading too much into it.

"Mary explained that this was normal."

I nodded. "Yeah. Just in my teens it was… I was a late bloomer and didn't have my bleeds until sixteen."

"That late?"

I nodded.

But I knew when she had her first. Unlike me, no pain. Barely even noticed their arrival until she felt the blood. I guess she hadn't changed.

"That must be why I don't remember helping you…" she trailed off.

"Yep," I confirmed. "If you need to take time off, you can," I told her. "Me like this isn't a special boss privilege."

"I'll keep it in mind."

We went to bed. She snuggled up to my back, placed her palm over my abdomen and rubbed soothing circles and I could've cried with how good it felt. Not just the hand. The hug. The fact she was there and whispering to me about what I'd missed in the shop. Making me laugh with her Easther impersonation.

"Um," I started.

"Hmm?"

"You don't have to be here..." I hated that I started saying those words. I cleared my throat. "If you want to spend the night in your room... it's fine. I'll be fine."

Her hand froze on my belly.

"Do you want to be alone?"

No.

I shook my head. "But I don't want you to think I expect this of you."

Her hand started to move again. She snuggled in close. "Don't be silly. I want to do this. I want to be here with you. If you'll have me."

I placed my hand over hers and pressed it harder into my stomach. "I want you here." *For as long as you stay.*

Seven months later...

"Are you alright?" I stroked the hair away from Isa's face.

She barely acknowledged the question. "Hmm." Just stayed where she was, head on my chest and fiddling with the quilt over the both of us.

"Isa?" I prodded her further.

"Hmm?"

"What's troubling you?"

Still nothing.

I huffed and took her chin into my hand and forced her to look up at me. "Isa."

She blinked and it was slow, like she was coming from far away, until she was able to focus her eyes upon me. "What?"

"What's wrong?" My hand tilted and I stroked my knuckles over her cheek.

She sighed. "It's the anniversary soon."

"Anniversary?" I asked. Wondering what she was going to be celebrating. She hadn't been my apprentice for a year yet... *oh. Oh!* "His passing?"

He nodded. "It'll be next month."

I didn't know what to say or how to comfort her, other than to go back to playing with her hair. Using my finger tips to scratch along her scalp gently. And just be there.

She moved her head so her face wasn't pointed my way, her ear pressed to my chest. I was grateful for that. I don't know what expression I was meant to be showing her.

Sympathy, sure. But… did she want sympathy? Did she need it? "Are you…" I started.

She said nothing to encourage me to continue.

"Are you wanting to go back? For the anniversary?"

I wasn't sure she'd heard me. Or that she registered that I had spoken at all. Long seconds drew out.

"I'm thinking about it," she finally admitted.

"Hmm," I grunted. Fell asleep like that. Not knowing fully what was agreed upon or how to offer support to her in this time. If she wanted it. Did she? It was her husband. The man she had loved and married and had children with. He left such a gap in her life.

And I was… her friend. Her boss. Her… friend.

*

Isa did take leave to return north to her family for the anniversary. She left one morning on the coach.

I went to work as normal.

It was fine. Everything was fine.

Easther talked. "My little sister is being so annoying," she complained. "She's thinking of getting an apprentice-ship. And what one do you think she's thinking of? A mantua maker. I tell her no. She's just… ugh! Una bambina! Too young!"

"How old is she?" Jane queried.

"Eleven."

Mary chuckled. "So young," she almost rolled her eyes. "A babe! Barely old enough to feed herself."

"Don't," Easther whined.

"You tease us all the time."

"Yes. But she's asking about working here with me. Even Mama is getting on my case and asking me to ask Anne. But I don't want mia sorella here with me. This is my escape. From that household!"

"Anne?" Mary looked over at me. "Do you have space for a new apprentice? It could be torture for Easther."

"Per favore, no!" Her hands welded together into a prayer position before her face. Eyes wide and begging.

I shook my head. "No."

Easther brightened up. She immediately threw her arms about my shoulders and peppered my cheeks with kisses. "Millie grazie, Anne!"

"Get off!" I snapped and batted her back with little slaps.

But still she persisted.

Mary snorted. "You had the perfect opportunity to torture her. Force her to mentor her own little sister."

"But then we'd have two of them here. And what if they started to fight? I can't. No," I finally forced Easther off of me and held her back at arm's length with a palm over her face. "Get back to work," I ordered her.

She babbled away in Italian. And with the way she was smiling, I guess it was grateful things she was saying.

I wasn't feeling indulgent at all. Didn't want to be sitting on the work table and chatting away with everyone else, or listen to them talk and have a good time.

"Are we not getting a new apprentice until either Easther or Isa finish?" Mary asked.

"Which of us is closer to finishing?" Easther jumped in. "Isa's been here for less than a year. But she has all of her previous experience. I've been here for almost five years. So I should be at the end soon."

"Maybe if you stopped flapping your lips, Anne would sign you off and you could set up your own shop and have your sister apprentice under you."

"Ack! Don't curse me!"

"I'm going to my office," I announced and slipped away. Their eyes on me as I closed the door. I knew they would be whispering. Probably saying something like 'Isa only just left this morning and Anne's already like this?'

The evening was awful.

I cooked and ate my meal alone. Silence. Sat in the sitting room with my knitting until it was a reasonable time to go to bed. And then nearly bawled my eyes out as I smelled Isa on the pillow.

One day and I was missing her. Like an ache in my chest and I hated it.

Two days.

Three.

A week passed.

That easy banter the others maintained as they worked disappeared. Or they just didn't engage me in it. Thank goodness.

I was spiky. Snapped at them.

Mary took care of the customers out front with Easther.

I stayed in my office mostly. Alone with my thoughts and wondered if Isa was going to come back. If she found she was more homesick and would stay instead. Pick up her apprenticeship with the same seamstress her daughter was under. Or maybe she would give up sewing completely and go back to the printing business of her husband's family.

She was a mother and her children were in the north. Why would she come back south?

She was someone's wife and his family were north.

Ugh! I slumped back into my chair and hated that… that I was alone and Isa was so far away. I missed her.

"Anne?" A knock on the door brought me out of my head.

"Hmm?"

It opened and showed Jane's worried little face. She bit her lip before saying. "Fanny is here."

I groaned. Perfect, just what I needed right now. Fanny.

Sulking for a second longer just because I could, I hauled myself up and out of the chair and followed Jane back into the world.

I met Fanny at the front counter. "Hello," I said. Nothing scathing and nothing to provoke her. I wanted this over and done with, with the least amount of interaction.

Mary cut a look at me. She stood beside me at the counter. Or I came to stand by her. Whatever. It didn't matter the order. I was here to deal with Fanny and settle the account for the month.

Fanny flicked her eyes up and down my body. "What's the matter with you?"

"Do you have our order?" I ignored her question, because no, I am not going to spill my guts to Fanny.

Mary, maybe. If I get out of this funk and open my mouth. Or have too much drink.

Fanny narrowed her eyes. "Did you lose another lover? That's what this is," she started to smirk. "Figures. You always get mopey when they leave you."

"The trim," my tone clip.

"Wasn't this one of your own apprentices?"

"Fanny. The order of trim."

"Thought you were smarter than to dilly dally with an employee."

"Your husband wasn't," I blurted out. "And that's why your last employee was able to steal all of your big clients and run off. And why your husband has been such an ass and been hassling the new shop girl you've employed, even though she has been clear that she wants none of him."

Fanny gaped. Flapped her lips as she tried to find some remark to come back at me with.

"The trim. Fanny."

She huffed and dumped the packets onto the bench.

In that tense air we settled the account for the month. She snatched the coin off of the counter and she turned on her heel to march out. Not before pausing to sneer back at me. "You're too emotional to be running a business!" She slammed the door. The bells overhead jingled violently.

I clenched my fists and wanted to scream at her!

"Anne," Mary spoke my name in her gentle mothering tone. Placed her hand to my shoulder.

I tried to shrug her off.

"Anne, talk to me."

"I'm fine," I snapped out.

"Isa is coming back."

"Why?" Came out before I could stop it. And it was the avalanche of words that followed that I wished to have kept to myself. "Why would she come back?! What is there for her to come back to? Her apprenticeship? She could pick one up anywhere. Hell, she should just be signed off and be called a mantua maker. Me? Is she going to come back for me? What am I to her? What if she wants to stay with her family? Or she meets another man? What if she only comes back to announce she's engaged again and isn't fin-ishing her apprenticeship and is going to get married and… and…" I gasped.

I was crying. Bawling my eyes out.

Mary bundled me to her chest and held me.

And it was too much of an echo of when she'd done that after Isa had left at sixteen. In the stairs leading up to the dorm and I'd broken down under Mary's concern. And without the others witnessing it, she'd pulled me into a hug in the darkened staircase and rubbed my back.

Only I hadn't been this emotional. I had been heartbro-ken, but I had thought I'd known where we stood and it had been silly for me to have cried over a girl I'd loved but had never loved me back.

Now… I love her again. I love this adult woman Isa. And she had been… with me… whatever we were. So…

I hiccupped and clung to Mary.

"She's coming back," Mary insisted.

"But for how long?"

She had no answer to that.

*

It was dark still when Isa came home. She'd slipped inside without me noticing, only disturbing me when she crawled under the covers and wrapped herself around me.

I turned. "Isa?"

"Hmm. I'm home," she said the words.

Even half asleep still, I wished for the hope not to flare up, to give me false expectation. But I curled around her. Buried my face into the crook of her neck. Held on tight.

Felt her take a shuddering breath and break.

"Shhh," I rubbed her back as she cried. "It's okay, love. I've got you. You're okay."

*

"Welcome back," Easther cried out when she saw Isa in her usual seat on the work table, cushion on her lap, and project draped over that. "We missed you!"

Isa smiled. It was still tinged with a melancholy that hadn't been there before. But it was still a smile, and I was grateful to see it again.

The chatter returned. Easther pestered Isa for gossip about her journey. What did she see? Was there any troubles?

Isa was all too happy to talk about her children. She produced a lovely new cap for her hair from her pocket. "My daughter made me this." Passed it over so everyone could inspect it's stitches and nod approvingly over them.

"How's she liking her apprenticeship?" Mary asked.

"She's loving it. The way she's improving shocks me. I'm so proud of her."

I came around and took the seat next to Isa, closest to the edge so I could get up to leave easily and attend to the front of shop should the door open. What I didn't expect was for Isa to fuss over me. She helped me to get situated and spread my project over my lap and handed me her scissors when I went looking for a pair.

All while still talking about her daughter.

Nothing too shocking, no. But then add in how she shuffled to be pressed against my side as we worked. Or how she offered to go and make me tea. Or the way she rested her head on my shoulder as she sighed and thought about something from her journey to share with Easther's eager questions.

"It's good you're back," Easther told her. "Anne really missed you."

I didn't scold her for tattling on me. Ignored her because I am an adult and she was little more than a brat.

"I missed Anne," Isa admitted aloud and before I could respond to that, swooped in and kissed me on the lips. A little peck.

My breath hitched. Eyes widened.

What was that?! In front of everyone?

"Aww, you're so adorable," Easther cooed. Pursed her lips and made obnoxious smooching noises.

Mary rolled her eyes and said nothing.

Jane blushed and looked everywhere but at us. As if she'd just seen her parents kissing.

I stared at Isa. She tossed her head back and cackled. "Don't look like that. Everyone knows already." To emphasise what they already were aware of, she threaded her fingers through mine and squeezed my hand. "It isn't a secret."

No, it wasn't.

But we'd never…

Not in front of everyone.

*

Next day, Isa kissed me again. This time when I'd thrown my cloak over my shoulders and grabbed my basket. "I'll be back soon," I'd told the workroom.

Isa had jumped up and hurried over to me. Her hands on my waist, she held me steady before kissing me. A farewell kiss. "See you soon," she said.

My face burned. I nodded and went out to do my business.

Coming back in, Isa repeated it. This time with a greeting kiss. "Did it all go well?" she asked.

And I promptly forgot all about what I'd gone out to do. Until Mary snatched the basket from me and searched through it for what she needed to finish off her order of two matching dresses for twin girls.

"Yes," I said. "Yes."

In the flat, Isa was worse. She combed my hair. Made me sit between her knees on the floor while she was on the bed. Combed it carefully. "I think I know what I want to do for my final assignment," she informed me.

"Isn't that something I get to decide and assign to you?"

She ignored that comment. "I want to make a gown for you."

"Me?" I tried not to whip my head around to look at her. "Why?"

She placed the comb to the side and slid her fingers into my hair, dividing it into sections and started to braid. "You made me a gown, remember?"

How could I forget? "Red."

"Hmm, and it was lovely. I loved it," she used her thighs to give my arms a squeeze as she said that. "And now I think it's time I made you one in return." Fixing off the end of the braid with a ribbon, she flicked it playfully over my shoulder.

I picked it up and looked at the ribbon. It was new. "Did you get this while in the north?"

"Yep. It was so pretty. But it was the end of the roll and only a little left."

I fingered it. "I like it," I said. Soft.

"I'm glad," she said back. "But the assignment."

"Why are you assuming you're finishing soon?"

"Because I'm at Mary's level."

"Don't let her hear that," I warned her.

"Why?"

"She'll laugh herself sick."

"Mary likes me."

"Hmm," I leaned my head to the side against her leg. It was soft. "They all like you."

Even though she'd just done my hair, she started to play with it. "What colour do you want for your gown?" her nails scratched along my scalp.

I frowned. "Do you want to finish your apprenticeship that fast?" I wondered. Heart clenching. Stomach in knots.

"Fast?"

I snorted. "Yeah, fast."

"I think you're forgetting the fourteen-year gap that I had."

"Of your own choosing," I forced a laugh into it so it wouldn't be mistaken as a stab. I didn't want to talk about this or think about what would happen if she was no longer an apprentice.

"I'm thinking green," she changed back to the fucking gown again.

I shook my head.

"Why not?" there was a pout in her voice.

"Don't like green. And too expensive."

"Then what do you want?"

"Something simple."

"It was always going to be simple. I would never force you into something you would hate to wear."

Ah! My heart. Stop with the attacks to my poor heart. Saying that you want to finish things but then showing that you know me… too much. It's making me feel too much.

And I needed to do something.

Without thinking of consequences, I turned and kissed the thigh I'd been resting against. Pushed the hem of the chemise up higher so I could mouth at the soft flesh there. Instead of asking her what she wanted to do after her apprenticeship. Put my mind at ease and having the fucking answers.

Isa twitched under my attentions. Her fingers dug into my hair. "Anne," she sighed. Purred. Lifted her legs and rested them onto my shoulders. Encouraged me on.

I spun onto my knees and buried my head between her legs. Revelled in the gasps and moans as I gave her pleasure with my mouth. Loved that she pushed my head in harder, rode my face with her hips bucking.

Thighs clamped over my ears as she came.

With a giggle, she lifted her chemise and peered down at me.

I blinked, now being able to see again. Liked what I saw. Kissed the crease between her hip and thigh. Laved at it with my tongue. Nipped with teeth. Wanted to leave a mark behind. Something for her to take with her when she would leave me. To prove that she had been loved by me.

"Come up here and let me take care of you," she demanded. Breathless.

Wiping her off of my mouth, I did as I was told. Crawled over her and kissed her and allowed her to force me to recline for her. "What are you going to do?" I asked her.

Isa kissed me. Messy. Laid her body onto mine, nestled between my legs and rocked her hips. "Gonna make you feel good," she whispered. "Gonna love you. Make you come for me."

I hooked my thigh up and over her hip, the heel of my foot digging into her rump and pressing her more firmly against me. "Promise?"

She lifted up and smirked at me. "Just lay back and be a good girl for me, hmm?"

I snorted at that. "And if I don't?"

She stuck her hand between us and started to play. All thought left me. She knew exactly what to do to me now. Sucked on my neck while she did. "Do as you're told," Isa chuckled.

8. My Heart on Your Sleeve

"What do you mean you're ending my apprentice-ship?" Isa jerked her head up from breakfast.

I took the seat across from her. "I'm saying you're a full fledge mantua maker now and no longer an apprentice." *And now you can leave.*

And I can get over it.

Isa frowned. "Really? That simple?"

"That simple," I focussed on my plate.

"But what about the gown?"

I shrugged. "Not necessary. You've proven your skill over and over. I'd be exploiting you if I didn't graduate you sooner rather than later." Sip of hot tea. Ah yes. Distracting as I burn my mouth.

Isa pouted. Pushed her food around her plate. Sighed.

"You don't want to be a mantua maker?" I asked.

"I want to make the gown." Stubborn.

"Why? It's a gown. I have several. Will just make myself one when I need a new one."

Isa glared at me. "That's not the point… ugh. I'm making you a gown!" she said with full force. "I don't care. I'm making it."

My heart clenched. "Okay," I conceded. "Thank you."

"Hmm," she hmphed. Then ignored me for the rest of the morning. Even when we both went down stairs, she didn't pay attention to me at all and went straight to her current project.

I announced to the others Isa's completion of her apprenticeship. They chorused with congratulations. Isa accepted it from all of them.

And still ignored me.

Which was fine.

It was dandy.

Getting ready for when she decides that she's going to head back north and be closer to her family. That's what this is. Break my heart a little here and the rest of it later. Get use to it. Just a teaser.

And I am a bloody coward and should just ask her what her plan is. I've cut the remaining tie and I am now waiting for her to tell me. When it would be better if I asked and knew what she wanted to do.

"When are you going to graduate me?" Easther pestered.

"When I hire your sister," I flat out taunted.

She gasped. "Rude!"

I felt the gap. Isa was sitting furthest away from me. Was chatting with Jane and not looking at me. *Ugh... this sucks.*

End of the day, after the shop closed and the others left, Isa didn't pack up.

"Strip," she ordered.

"Excuse me?"

"Strip. I'll get the draping done while you're still willing to accept a gown from me," she snapped.

"It's not that I don't want one..."

"Then why is the idea of me making something for you so terrible in your mind?" She planted her hands to her hips and glared at me.

"Because," I had nothing. I inhaled and inflated my cheeks as I held it in and waited. Still nothing came. It isn't necessary for her to make me anything. She owes me nothing. I owe her wages. I don't need a new gown.

She reached over and pressed her palms over my cheeks and forced the air out in a raspberry. Making us both lose it and giggle.

I sighed. "I don't know. It's odd to have someone making me things." There. Admitted.

"Haven't other apprentices done that?"

I shrugged.

"Or is it because it's me?"

Oh. I didn't respond and she had her answer.

Isa held me in place. "Listen to me, Anne. I am making this dress because I want to make you something. It's special because it's coming from me for you. You made me a gown that I cherished and wore until I no longer could fit into it."

I blinked at her.

"And I don't expect you to have the same sentimental hold on a garment, but it means a lot for me to give a gown back to you."

Shit. My eyes started to water. "Isa," I said.

She swept in and pecked my lips. "So strip and stand still."

We laughed at that. I did as I was told and got down to my under garments, stood still in the middle of the workroom as she started to work. Draped large chunks of fabric to my chest and back and hacked away the bulk of it until she got it closer to the sizing and shaping she desired.

"There's a nice patterned cotton," I ventured.

"Is that what you want?"

I tried not to shrug and disrupt her scissors. Especially when they were against my skin at my neckline. "It's leftover from a client's gown a while back. Was going to give it to Jane to play with."

"But is it what you want?" she repeated.

And I had to swallow hard. *What the hell was this? What I wanted?* It felt like she was meaning more than just the fucking fabric she would use for a gown that was for me. Like she was asking more personally. But…

I had a lot. I had my independence, thanks to my business. I had friends I cared for. I bit my lip and looked at the crown of Isa's head, at the wildness that was escaping her pins at the end of the day.

I wanted her. To stay. I wanted Isa to stay.

And I don't want to be the reason why she does.

It's stupid.

I don't want to say to her, to stay, because I wanted her. And then for her to stay because I asked. I wanted her to stay because she wanted to be there. Or to leave and go and do what it was that she needed to in her life.

I wanted her to stay only if she wanted to.

But I'm not opening my damn mouth and asking what she wants. I'm just standing in my stays with fabric pinned to them, and the woman I love shaping a bodice for a gown that she's so bloody insistent on making for me.

What the devil was wrong with me?

"Blue."

"Hmm?"

"Blue. I want a blue gown."

Isa tilted her chin and smiled at me. "Now was that so hard to tell me?"

YES! Yes it bloody well was! All of it being torturous inside of my head. I rolled my eyes at her. "We don't have any blue on hand in the store."

"Then I guess we're just going to have to order some," she straightened up and placed her hands on my hips and turned me to face the mirror. "Now, I like it a little lower here," she reached around and traced the neckline on me. Pressed the mock up piece inches lowers than where she'd done her rough cut in.

I pulled a face, a 'really?'

She grinned at me in the reflection. "Higher?" she dragged the digit up until finally her touch transferred to skin. Touched my collarbone. "Or lower?" and then she dipped her fingers low again, this time under the fabric, to the edge of my stays. Under my stays. As far as she could get them.

"Get me out of this," I ordered.

She hurried to unpin. Hurried to keep it in order while I vibrated and wanted to tear it all away.

The last piece and pin out of the way, I attacked. Grabbed her and hauled her to press against my body. Kissed her rough and messy.

It hadn't even been at all that much of a build up with her fingering my chest. So why was I losing it so much?

Why was she meeting me back with equal vigour?

Didn't matter.

What mattered was getting Isa on the work table. I bent her backwards and guided her down so she laid on her back. Began to move down, only for her hands to haul me back up. Kissed me more.

"Love," I panted into her mouth. "Let me."

She shook her head. "No. I like it when we do it together."

"Fuck," that was hot.

Then I was changing plans. "Sit up for me." Climbed up fully onto the work table and grabbed the cushions. Stuffed them under my knees. "Come here." Made her straddle my lap.

She was taller like this. Wrapped her arms over my shoulders and allowed her hands to dive into my hair. She tilted my head and held me captive with her lips and her tongue.

I moaned and bucked up into her. Had her rut down into me.

She broke the kiss. Moved erratic and desperate. "Anne, please," she begged. "Tell me what we're doing."

Instead of telling, I licked my fingers and hauled her skirts up enough to slip under. Shit, she was still fully dressed. "Do the same to me," I told her.

She followed suit, only having to go under my petticoats.

We fingered each other. My head dropped to her shoulder, turned and I laid sloppy kisses to her throat. Right over her throbbing pulse.

Her hips bucked. She moaned and her free hand pressed harder on the back of my head.

Heaven… doesn't even compare.

*

The blue fabric came in a week later. Isa worked on the gown in between client's work. She grinned as she did so. Would tell everyone about the project, even though they already knew about it. In detail. As if she was a child showing off their favourite toy.

I was tempted to sabotage the dress. If she never finished, she would never leave.

Yet again, that wasn't what I wanted to do to her. So, I watched as she put it together. As she pleated the skirt. Whip stitched the seams.

Until she was finished.

"Try it on," Isa insisted.

"It looks good," I commented as I picked it up to inspect. But she stopped me from doing that and pushed on my shoulder to force me to the bedroom.

"Try it on," she repeated.

"After I've cleaned up."

It was the end of the day. I'd been on my feet in the front of the shop with clients doing final fittings. I just wanted to wash and collapse for an hour before even contemplating food.

"Please," she begged.

"I don't want to get it dirty just by trying it on," I complained.

This time, she reached out and began to undress me. "I'll help."

"Are you helpful?" I tried to tease, but it came out tired. Sighing, I relented and allowed her to help me out of my working gown and then slip into her new one.

And it was… wow. She'd made this for me. Special. Made me want to be extra careful of it. Not to wear it at all, just bundle it up and squirrel it away.

Simple, yes. And I loved that. Neckline higher than was fashionable, as I enjoyed it. Fitted bodice and sleeves. A beautiful blue.

She tugged me this way and that. Got me into the skirts. Fussed.

"Lovely. You look lovely," she said.

I twisted my wrist to start inspecting what I could and to give her praise on her workmanship. I paused. Frowned. Looked closer.

Embroidered on the inner wrist of the left sleeve was a heart. Two initials inside of it. *I+A.*

Oh Lord.

Oh.

She bit her lip and looked at me expectantly. "I was being sentimental," she admitted.

I was frozen.

"Anne?"

...

"So?" she tried to prompt me. Fidgeted with the gown on me. "What do you think?"

"Mercy," I whispered.

"Pardon?"

"Please, have mercy," I broke and started to cry.

Isa gathered me into her arms and held me tight. "Anne, hush. What's all of this? Anne!" she said it with more force to try and get me to answer when all I could do was collapse into her and cry.

My added weight to her dragged her to the floor with me. The skirts now getting dirty from it.

"Please, Anne. You're scaring me."

"I love you," I sobbed.

"I love you, too."

"No. I mean. Ugh! I love you and I want you to stay but I don't want to force you to stay just because I want it. But you're going to want to go back to your family in the north. Or meet someone else and leave me and get married again. Or..." I gasped hard. Unable to breathe with the amount of snot I was producing.

Shit.

I shuddered with an inhale. "Isa, have mercy on my heart."

Like a bloody mother, she produced a handkerchief from thin air and wiped my tears. Held it to my nose and made me blow. "You fool," she snapped at me. "You stupid bloody fool."

"Why are you scolding me?" I sniffled and still cried.

"Because, idiot, I love you. And I want to stay! I want to stay with you! I don't want to marry again. I only want to be with you Anne, until you're sick of me and even after that."

And then she kissed me.

Through the snot and tears, she kissed me and held me. And I kissed her back. Breaking it to gasp for air and having to grab her handkerchief and blow my nose. Laughing with her at how ridiculous it all was.

*

I told her all of my insecurities. Under duress. She threatened me until I admitted it all. Then berated me again for not talking to her. Only to make sure I knew how she felt by showering me in love. All night.

*

"If you get another apprentice, will you include board?" Easther asked.

"No," Isa answered.

"Why not?"

"We have no room," she answered truthfully.

"But don't you two share a bed?"

"We do."

"Don't go telling her things," I warned.

Isa and Easther ignored me.

"So there's a free room for you to put another apprentice," Easther insisted.

"Still no room. And do you really think an apprentice wants to hear us at night. The walls are thin." And with that, Isa had silenced the workroom.

Easther gaped, realisation dawning over her face, followed by rapid fire Italian and then her crossing herself.

Jane slapped her hands over her ears and groaned.

Mary snorted.

And I sighed and looked at my beloved. "Well, you're amazing."

She grinned back at me. "Not quite. She's still talking." And then we dissolved into giggles and leaned into each other.

Hello,

Thank you for reading. I hope you enjoyed My Heart on Your Sleeve.
I would much appreciate it if you did leave an honest review wherever you like to leave reviews.
If you would like to read more head to
aprilklasenbooks.weebly.com
Happy reading,
April

Independently published author. Artist. BL and fanfic whore. April Klasen lives in regional NSW Australia. Find her @defiantdame on most social media sites or sign up for the book newsletter.

More books are coming.

Also by April Klasen

Romance:
My Heart on Your Sleeve
I Don't Like Coffee, I Like You
Fitz: A Queer Pride & Prejudice Retelling
Pure Pop Asia
I Heart Pop Asia
Summertime Madness
Hook-up or Date

Fantasy:
A Witch's Wand
The Annual
Beta
Blair: Salem's Daughter
Blair: The Sleeping Daughter
Blair: The Same Daughter

www.ingramcontent.com/pod-product-compliance
Lightning Source LLC
Chambersburg PA
CBHW070445170726
48291CB00005B/1599